TEMPTED BY THE COWBOY

Cowboy Dreamin' 4

Sandy Sullivan

Erotic Romance

Secret Cravings Publishing
www.secretcravingspublishing.com

A Secret Cravings Publishing Book
Erotic Romance

Tempted by the Cowboy
Copyright © 2014 Sandy Sullivan
Print ISBN: 978-1-63105-217-0

First E-book Publication: March 2014
First Print Publication: May 2014

Cover design by Dawné Dominique
Edited by Stephanie Balistreri
Proofread by Rene Flowers
All cover art and logo copyright © 2014 by Secret
Cravings Publishing

PUBLISHER
Secret Cravings Publishing
www.secretcravingspublishing.com

Dedication

To all my fans out there, I love you dearly and I
hope you enjoy the next installment
of the Cowboy Dreamin' series.

TEMPTED BY THE COWBOY

Sandy Sullivan
Copyright © 2014

Chapter One

Peyton Matthews stood at the edge of the crowd watching as the Young brothers did their best to sling mud in every direction. Muddin'. The cowboy way of having fun on a hot early summer evening. A little dirt, a lot of water, some big mud tires on a pickup truck, and you had yourself a grand time in Bandera, Texas.

She wasn't sure why she let Aaron talk her into coming to this tonight. The cowboy way of life came hard for her. With her multiple tattoos, piercings, and loner mentality, she really didn't fit in here. Even as a child, she'd been out of place with her tomboyish attitude. She hadn't grown into her female body until later in high school as she cursed every curve, swell and period from then on. Not that she didn't like being a woman now, but she sure hadn't during puberty. And when the boys started noticing she had boobs? Oh boy! The gloves came off. Several of them got bloody noses from a well-placed fist.

Next up, the infuriating Jason Young, who took his turn at the hole. Mud flew in several directions, coating the crowd watching with the sticky substance. His red truck took the brunt of the splash, slinging the dirt over the entire side.

The grin he flashed from the driver's seat was infectious and she couldn't help but smile in return. He sure did have a pretty smile. Not that she really noticed or anything.

She knew his type. She'd seen it several times over the last several months as he played each female in The Dusty Boot like a fiddle with the strings too tight. A different one each time he came in.

As one of the bartenders who worked the joint, she saw him a lot. More than she wanted to, most of the time. She couldn't help but notice the way he carried himself. Nor, could she take her eyes off the cut of his shirt over the muscles of his chest, the snug way his jeans molded to his nice ass and those lips. God help her, those lips. Dark, thick hair hung to his collar with a slight wave. Her fingers itched to run through those strands.

A slight shift in her stance relieved some of the pressure on her clit, just not enough to satisfy the ache building. Maybe she'd let Aaron have a go tonight. She glanced toward where he sat reclining against a hay bale with a long-neck beer between his fingers in one hand and a cigarette clutched between his teeth. Okay, maybe not. Why she even went out with the guy, she didn't know other than she didn't want to spend another Saturday night off, sitting at home watching reruns of Will and Grace.

She sipped her beer, grimacing at the taste. The malty liquid had the ability to make her stomach lurch. Give her a shot of whiskey and water before the taste of this shit, any day, but it was liquor. Right now she needed the bite of alcohol on her tongue.

Today sucked. The whole thing from morning until now bit the big one. Memories had swamped her most of all, bringing down her mood into the pits of hell.

One year ago today, her mother had passed away from breast cancer. She took another sip from the bottle in her hand. *Yuck!* She tossed it into the trash can to her left before she stuffed her hands into her back pockets.

Jason took another run at the hole as she shook her head. The man knew what to do to make himself visible. Again, he probably had to being one of the Young triplets, identical triplets at that, although she had always been able to tell them apart when she'd had the privilege of gazing into their gorgeous faces. The other two weren't quite as broad across the shoulders as Jason. Something lingered in his gaze too. She wasn't sure what, but it intrigued her. Something wild. Something untamed maybe.

They all had the sweetest dimpled grin, but Jason seemed to have the half crooked tilt to his lips down pat. Boy did it work on the ladies.

She scuffed the toe of her boot in the dirt as she sighed heavily. It wouldn't do a bit of good to get tangled up with the likes of him even if he might be available. He wasn't as far as she knew. She didn't necessarily keep up with his whereabouts or latest fling. Well that's what she told herself anyway even if she noticed every girl he came in with or went home with. *Damn.*

"Hey, babe. Why don't you sit here with me," Aaron said, patting the hay bale next to him.

"No thanks."

"What's wrong?"

"Nothing. Why?"

"You came with me, you know."

"I know I did, Aaron, but don't pull your macho shit with me. I can find another way home. There are plenty of people from town here I could hitch a ride with."

"Like one of the Young boys?" He climbed to his feet, swaying slightly. "Don't think I haven't seen you watchin' several of them tonight."

He grabbed her arm, but she yanked it out of his hold. "Don't manhandle me, jackass."

"Aw, come on, babe. I don't wanna fuss with you. I wanna love on you."

"Yeah, not happenin'."

"Problem?" Jason stepped out of the shadows of the tree line.

Her breath stopped in her throat as it closed off. "No problem." The words came out in a squeak, not at all what she'd hoped to sound like—confident in her ability to take care of herself.

"Back off, Young."

"Fuck you, Scarborough. You don't get rough with a woman while I'm around."

"She ain't your woman."

"She isn't yours either, asshole." He touched her arm where Aaron had grabbed. "Are you okay, Peyton?"

"I'm fine. Thanks." She tipped her head back slightly to look down her nose at the idiot she came with. Big mistake, but one she'd own up to. "I can handle him."

"I'm sure you can, darlin', but you don't have to."

"It's okay."

"If you need a ride back to town later, let me know. As for now, have a good time."

He walked away, taking his scent and the heat of his hand with him. Goose bumps rose on her arms. The urge to calm them with her hands, flittered across her shoulders. She ignored the urge, almost embracing the affect he had on her as desire coiled low in her belly.

Aaron burped loudly. "You aren't his type, you know."

"What are you yammering about now?"

"Jason." He pointed with the bottle in his hand as he took a drag on his cigarette. "You aren't his type. He wants a downhome country girl, not a tattooed up, rough around the edges chick like you."

"I don't care what his *type* is." She shrugged as she glanced down at the nails on her left hand. "I'm not looking to hook up with any of the Young boys."

"Good. Come here then." He jerked her into his arms, effectively caging her in his tight embrace.

The wet slide of his lips along her neck almost made her gag. The inclination doubled as she glanced across the clearing straight into the glittering blue gaze of Jason. The frown pulling down the corners of his mouth made her frown in return. "I don't want this, Aaron."

She pushed him back by the shoulders.

"What the fuck, babe? I know you're horny. I can smell it on you."

"I'm not horny for you."

"Bitch!" He slapped her hard across the cheek, tossing her to the ground at his feet. "You fucking cunt. You aren't good enough for the likes of me. I wouldn't fuck you if you were the last pussy in Bandera."

Within seconds, Jason had him by the front of his shirt as he lifted him until his feet dangled. "I told you, you don't hurt a woman while I'm around." Jason pulled back his fist and proceeded to punch Aaron in the nose. Hard. He landed two more before two of his brothers hauled him off even though he struggled in their hold. "Let go. I'm gonna make sure he never hits a woman again while I mess up his pretty face."

"He's not worth the trouble, bro." Joel held one arm while Jackson had the other.

Jason shook off their hands.

"Fuckin' bastard! You're gonna be sorry you did this," Aaron threatened as he struggled to his feet.

Jason lunged, but his brothers grabbed him before he could do any further damage. "Get the fuck off our property, Scarborough. Don't ever come back or there will be nine of us against one of you."

Aaron held his nose, making his voice come out in a deep nasally sound. "You don't own the God damn county, Young. I can do what I want."

"Not on our property." Jason glanced at her as she struggled to her feet. "You okay?"

"Yeah."

He touched her cheek with his fingertips. "You'll probably have a bruise tomorrow."

She winced from the scrape of his calluses. "I'm sure." She dropped her gaze from connecting with his. She never could handle looking deep into his eyes. The color of a clear lake somewhere in the mountains, she'd always melted into a puddle of goo when they connected. "Thanks for sticking up for me."

"I'd do it for anyone."

Ouch. "Thanks anyway. I appreciate it."

Nina, Jason's mother, came to her side. "Are you all right, Peyton?" She looked at the boys who'd begun to gather. "Get him off the property. I don't care how to you do it, but I want him out of here."

Jeremiah and Jackson grabbed Aaron by the arms none too gently and pushed him toward where his car sat off to the back of the packed group.

"I'm fine, Nina, but thank you."

"Don't thank me, honey. I didn't do anything. You should be more careful who you keep company with."

"I know. Trust me, I won't be keeping company with him again. I won't tolerate a man hitting me. If Jason hadn't stepped in, I would have decked him myself."

Nina laughed. "I get the impression you can take care of yourself most of the time."

Peyton nodded as she touched her fingertips to her cheek. "I can." She sighed when she dropped her hand back to her side. "I guess I should find someone to take me home."

"I will." Jason took out his keys. "Just say when."

"You know, I think I'll stay awhile. I'm not going to let one asshole ruin my afternoon. Let the mud sling, baby!"

Jason laughed. The sound rippled down her back in a slow shiver. He pulled her in for a quick hug.

"I like you, Peyton Matthews. How about you take a run with me through the mud?"

"Run?"

"Yeah. You came to get down and dirty, didn't you?" he asked, his hands on his hips. One eyebrow cocked over his eye right before a panty-melting grin spread across his lips. He dove for her, pressing his shoulder into her abdomen as he lifted her off the ground before he strolled for the mud pit.

She reached down to smack his taut ass, realizing just how tight his butt was. *Holy hell!* Her long hair swung back and forth, blocking her vision as the catcalls flew.

"Get her, Jason."

"Hey, Peyton. Takin' a bath with Jason?"

She felt her face flush hot. "Put me down."

"Nope."

His boots hit the edge of the mud pit, with both feet sliding until they went down into the water. He'd tried to bring her back over his shoulder before they landed, only to hit a dirt mound in the middle. This caused him to lose his grip until she landed directly on top of him, her face to his crotch and her legs cradling his head. The crowd roared. Jason laughed and she couldn't help but laugh too no matter the precarious place her face brushed against.

The shape of his cock stood proud, outlined by the tight wetness of his jeans.

"Havin' a good time down there?"

"What? Shit." She scrambled off him to land butt first in the mud.

The whole crowd got into it by jumping into the pit with them. A huge mud fight ensued with everyone throwing globs of sludge at each other until the entire group stood dripping from head to toe.

The parental unit stood on the sidelines laughing until they bent over at the waist.

Peyton crawled toward the edge, only to be pulled back in by her boot. When she twisted around, Jason was grinning at her like a fool. Dirt smudged his cheeks and dripped from his hair as his shirt lay plastered to his chest.

"Where do you think you're going?"

"Out?"

"Nope." He dragged her back in until they were stuck in the middle of the dirt party again. Someone pushed him from behind, propelling him toward her until she thought he'd land directly on her, drowning her in the process. Right before he landed, he braced himself with his arms so he didn't squash her, but it brought them in close proximity from nose to toes.

She lost herself in his eyes until he slowly bent his head, closing the distance between them for what she really hoped to be a light-me-on-fire kiss.

Right before he brought their mouths together, one of his brothers tackled him, throwing him off of her. *Damn it!* She pushed herself to her elbows, grimacing as the mud squished under the pressure. She laughed as she watched the entire crowd sling mud every which direction at each other.

Two of the Young brothers grabbed their parents to drag them into the fray. Everyone got into it, even the wives or girlfriends of the boys already paired up. Mesa jumped in with both feet, Terri threw a big mud ball at Jeff, and Paige pushed Jacob down even though he took her with him into the mud. They seemed like such a happy family. All of them. Something she wished she'd had growing up.

Her mother had been a single parent from the time of her father took off when she was a child. She'd never had siblings so she didn't know how to act around a lot of people sometimes. She'd always felt it must have been her fault her father left. He didn't love her…didn't want her or something. She'd only been two when he'd taken a business trip and never came back. She didn't want to find him, never wanting to know the truth behind why he took off like he did. Her mother didn't discuss him. There were never any pictures. She didn't even know what he looked like anymore.

Enough feeling sorry for myself. I'm going to enjoy this time with a family even if I'm not part of it.

The party died down as everyone worked their way out of the mud pit and started for their vehicles to head home. The sun started to go down over the horizon, bringing with it the inky blackness of the night way too soon. The Youngs usually had a bonfire with their muddin' parties, but since everyone was head to toe in mud, they decided to forgo it this time and have one at the house should anyone want to clean up before they came by.

"I'll take you home to change if you want to come back for the bonfire."

"I would appreciate the ride, but I don't think I'll come back."

"Why not?" Jason asked, wiping a smear of mud from her cheek.

"Even though it was a lot of fun hanging out with your family, I just don't fit in with the family thing."

"Sure you do. You'd get along great with Mesa and Terri. Isn't Paige one of your friends?"

"Yes."

"Then there you go. You'd fit right in."

She cocked an eyebrow. "Really? I'm not the good little girl, perfect housewife and mother type."

"Good. I kind of like the wild ones."

She braced her hands on her hips. "Are you coming onto me, Jason Young?"

"Is it workin' 'cause I can really turn on the charm if it's not." He grinned as she laughed.

"I'd be obliged if you'd take me home."

"Sure enough, darlin'. Let me change clothes and I'll be happy to take you." They walked to his truck in silence as she took in the mud slung all over the sides.

"How do you keep the mud from getting inside when you're all muddy yourself?"

"I have blankets to put on the seats until I get home, but they are leather so it's a quick wipe off anyway." He grabbed the blanket out from behind the seats to spread it out.

"Good thinking." He helped her into the jacked up truck with a hand on her butt. When she turned around to scold him, he just grinned. She rolled her eyes. Being mad at that handsome face wouldn't go very far so she didn't try.

Once he sat behind the wheel, the engine roared to life with a distinctive growl that settled low in her belly. She loved the rumble of a diesel engine.

They pulled out, bouncing along the rutted road until they made it to one of the ranch gates where he could get out onto the small highway. "We'll head back to my place so I can change."

"Sounds fine." She wasn't sure she could handle being in his house while he changed clothes and not jump him. All the looks he was giving her had her wound tight and ready to bust loose. If she could just get home without him touching her, she could relieve some of the pressure with her friendly battery operated boyfriend until she could possibly scope out someone else. *Why don't I bust this dry spell with him? I'm sure if I propositioned him, he'd be willing. A one night stand with a handsome cowboy wouldn't be so bad, right?*

Within minutes, they were pulling through a side gate of the ranch she hadn't known existed.

"You live out here?"

"Yeah. I built this place over the last couple of years."

They pulled up slowly toward a wood frame, two story log cabin. "Even though you don't have a wife or steady girlfriend?" *Wow. It's beautiful!*

"Yep. I used to stay in one of the bedrooms upstairs in the main lodge, but it got kind of noisy with the tourists, so I got me a log cabin kit. I've been building on it. The outside is finished, but I don't have any landscapin' or anything. It's not finished on the inside yet, although I have my bedroom and bathroom done."

"You're living out here then?"

"Yeah. I'm slowly doing things when I have time away from my duties at the ranch. Do you want to see the inside?"

"No!" She cleared her throat. "I mean, no. I'm head to toe in mud. I don't want to get your floors dirty or anything."

"You could shower here and I could wash your clothes."

Wow, the opportunity to have Jason Young all to herself in his house almost overwhelmed her. No other women around. No one hanging on his every word.

"What do you say? I'll even share the shower with you if you want."

"Oh you are so tempting."

"I only want what is best for both of us, darlin'. When you have clean clothes and showered, we can go back to the bonfire. No hanky panky unless you are feelin' the burn."

"What if I say yes?"

"To what?"

"All of it. I wouldn't mind ridin' you like a wild stallion."

His sexy-ass grin reappeared. "If you are propositioning me, babe, I'm ready, willing and able to take care of your needs all the way around the clock if you want to."

"Let's check out your bathroom then and we'll see where it leads."

The moment the engine cut, he was around the passenger side of the truck, pulling the door open with a yank. He scooped her up from her seat into his arms, hurrying for the cabin. "Uh, you forgot to shut the door."

"Crap." He walked back and used her booted foot to push it closed.

Seconds later, he fumbled with the key to the door lock. "Let me." She took the keys from his hand to open the door. Even though the house wasn't finished, what he had done amazed her. A large stone fireplace encompassed one wall to her left. Although it wasn't lit currently with the warmer temperatures of the early summer months in Bandera, she could see him sitting in front the flames reading a book. Okay, maybe not reading a book, but reclining in his naked glory on a fluffy rug just waiting for a woman to rub him all over.

She blinked as he set her down on her feet.

"Strip it off, babe."

"Right here?" she asked as he plucked a couple of buttons loose down the front of her shirt.

"Yeah. I mean this way we won't carry the mud through the house and I can put your clothes in the washer right now."

Self-consciousness swamped her. This would be the first time he'd see her naked and she wasn't sure what he'd think. She wasn't slender like a lot of women. She had curves, bulges and even some cellulite. What about her tattoos and piercings? Would he find them sexy or disgusting? She covered her breasts with her hands.

"What's wrong?"

"I've never undressed in front of you before."

"I know." He grinned. "I can't wait to see what treasures you're hidin' under there."

"How do you feel about tats?"

"I love them. I have two myself."

"You do?"

"Yeah. I have a band around my left bicep and a tribal swirl around my right shoulder and chest." He pulled his shirt out of the waistband of his jeans, then eased each button down the front from its hole, one by one.

Her breath caught in her throat as the spit in her mouth dried up like the Mohave Desert. She was going to finally see the fine pecs of Jason Young. The man she'd fantasized over for the last several months.

When he pulled the shirt from his shoulders, she caught her bottom lip between her teeth. *Dayum!*

"You like?"

Without realizing it until she touched his chest, she had reached her hand out to trace the swirling black along his pec. "Nice. It suits you."

"Thanks."

She glanced at the band around his bicep, noting the simplistic design of the silver spur brand entwined in the ink. "You have the ranch brand in there."

"Yeah. The ranch means everything to me, probably more than any woman ever will."

"Not makin' points here, cowboy."

"Sorry, but I figured you should know up front, I'm not lookin' for a wife."

"Good. I'm not lookin' for a husband."

He worked the buttons on her shirt until it hung loose at her waist. She'd worn a chemise top underneath with the sleeves cut off and a pair of jeans to the party.

"So where are yours?"

"I have a few."

"Where?"

"My ankle. My shoulder blade. One above my breast for my mother who died of breast cancer last year."

"I'm so sorry," he said in a soft whisper as he brushed his lips against her temple.

No one had ever moved her as deeply as he did with that simple touch. "It's okay. She'd been sick a long time. Even beat it once, but it came back with a vengeance. Brain cancer finally took her life in the end."

He worked the shirt from her arms, dropping it at her feet in a heap. "Toe off your boots so you can shed those jeans."

"I think you're just trying to get me out of my clothes, mister."

"Is it workin'?" he asked with a grin.

"Seems to be," she said, glancing down at her slowly building pile of clothes at their feet.

"Good." He unbuckled her belt and pushed down the zipper until her pants gaped at the waist, then fell to the floor. "Step out."

She complied blindly. Why, she wasn't sure other than she'd had it bad for this man for some time and if it meant taking the bull by the horns this one chance, she'd do it in heartbeat. Before she could change her mind, she lifted her chemise over her head, exposing her complete nakedness to his roaming gaze.

"You're beautiful."

"I bet you say that to every girl you have naked in your house."

"Nope, since you're the only woman who's been naked in this house with me."

"Really?" *He's never had a woman here before?*

"Yes."

"The sexy Jason Young? Hmm."

"Believe it or not, I haven't had a woman here before." He glanced around before his gaze came back to her. "This is my space. My sanctuary so I don't usually bring women here."

"Why me? Why now?"

"You're special and I want to help you. Nothin' says anything has to happen between us unless you want it to. Really, I only brought you here so you could shower and I could wash your clothes. You seemed like you were having a good time at the muddin' and didn't want it to be over. This was a way to keep the night from ending." He slowly traced the heart tattoo on her upper breast. "This is nice. Kind of a tribute."

"Yeah."

He stepped back.

"Aren't you going to strip too?"

"Yep."

"Right here?"

One eyebrow lifted. "Care to watch?"

"Oh hell yeah."

She admired his chest again. He sure was pretty to look at. Next, came the pants. Without preamble, he unbuckled and unzipped his jeans, pushing them to the floor in a whoosh. "Sweet mother of God," she murmured when his cock sprang free.

With a quick spin, he headed down the hall, assuming she would follow blindly. How could she not with his tight ass jiggling slightly as he walked.

"Come on. I'll show you the bathroom before I throw your clothes in the washer."

Even though he said the inside of the house wasn't done, most of his personal space was. They walked by the kitchen with its hickory cabinets and stainless steel appliances, to the next doorway at the end of the hall. It opened to reveal his bedroom. The deep grey on the walls complimented the dark furniture expertly. A burgundy red comforter graced the bed with deep pillow softness she wanted to sink into and never come out.

"The bathroom is through here."

With a flick of the switch, he illuminated the beautiful bathroom. "My God, Jason. This is gorgeous."

Travertine tiles graced the floor, but it was warm to the bottom of her feet.

"Radiant heat."

"Wow."

A huge shower sat in the back corner with a big rain type showerhead, glass walls, and silver accents. "The shower has several jets so you can get water everywhere."

"This is beautiful. You sure went all out."

He shrugged as pink stained his cheeks. *A blush?*

"What can I say, I like my luxury in the bathroom."

Her gaze kept bouncing from one thing to another as she tried to take it all in. "I'd say. I haven't seen a bathroom this nice in a long time. Usually at a high end hotel or something."

He pointed to the floor to ceiling cabinet to their left. "There are towels in the cupboard. Shampoo and soap in the shower. Take your time. I'll find you something to wear until your clothes are washed. It'll take about forty-five minutes in the washer and half an hour in the dryer probably."

She pressed her lips together for a moment. "Thank you. You don't know how much this means to me. I really never thought I'd be here with you like this when this evening started out."

His lips quirked up in a half smile. "You're welcome. Take your time. I'll use the other bathroom."

"What? Wait! No, I'll use the other bathroom. You use yours." She stepped toward him. "I'm not going to take your bathroom from you."

"I insist. Use it. I need to get other things together before I can get in."

She captured her bottom lip between her teeth. "Maybe you'd like to join me?"

Chapter Two

Jason sighed. *I'm actually going to walk away from having sex with one of the hottest women in Bandera. Yeah, damn it!* "You know, darlin', I would love to."

"But?"

"I don't think now is the right time for you and me."

"Why not?"

"It would be just sex."

"Yeah and?"

"I don't want to use you like that."

"Neither of us is looking for a relationship at the moment, right?"

"True."

One sharp fingernail skimmed down his chest. "Then what's wrong chasing away the lonely night with someone we are attracted to?" She glanced down at his erect cock. "I assume you are attracted to me."

His cock bobbed in agreement. "Not just yeah, but hell yeah."

She encircled his left nipple with the sharp end of her nail. His whole body went on high alert as shivers rolled from the top of his head to the tips of his toes.

Hot didn't do her justice. Brown eyes sparkled with mischief as a small smile curved her lips at the corners. Her breasts were high and full, plenty for a man's hand. Long, light brown hair brushed the curve of her waist. A waist that dipped in, not sharply like a stick model thin woman's, but gracefully like she wasn't afraid to eat. He groaned silently at the thought of those willowy legs wrapped around his waist as he sank into her heat.

Getting tangled in the sheets with her sounded like an *awesome* idea. Unfortunately for his willing cock, tonight wasn't the night. For some crazy-ass reason, he wanted to let the sexual tension build like the pressure of a volcano before he let it loose on the beauty standing in front of him.

"Make no mistake, baby. I want you. I want you bad, but I'm not going to take advantage of the situation. When we fuck for the first time, it's gonna be mind-blowing. Tonight ain't the night." His cock ached for the tight wetness he would find between her gorgeous thighs when he stepped back and left the bathroom with a click of the door.

He released a tortured, frustrated sigh as he leaned against the door jam. *Why did I think denying myself the pleasure of her body was a good idea?*

"Because in the end, it'll be worth it."

He dejectedly pulled himself away from the door before heading down the hall toward the other bathroom. After a minute, he reversed direction to grab their clothes from the front hall to throw them in the washer. He hoped she didn't require her unmentionables to be hand washed or anything. Like any typical bachelor, everything went into the washer together after he poured soap in the dispenser. A quick turn on the dial had the washer filling with water. He chuckled. She might end up with pink underwear should he do anything fancy with them.

"Shower." He picked the dried dirt from his hair as he walked back down the hallway to the second bathroom. When he'd finished it, he never really thought he'd be the one using it. Not this soon anyway.

The inside of the house had only been done for a few months and he still had a ton to do. Kitchen, two other bedrooms, his game room, and another barn needed to be built to house his animals. Like his father before him, he planned on running cattle on his piece of property as well as breeding bucking bulls. He wasn't so much into the rodeo thing as a rider, but he sure wanted to cash in on the lucrative business of bucking bulls for the Professional Bull Riders Association.

He snapped his fingers. *Damn, the shampoo is all in the master bathroom.* He switched directions again to get some stuff to shower with, hoping the shower stall door would be totally steamed up so he wouldn't have to see the gorgeous woman gracing his shower.

No such luck.

The minute he opened the bathroom door, he was struck by the silhouette of her. Each curve made his mouth water. His fingers itched to touch. He wanted to skim his palm along the slope of her breast.

She tipped her head back to rinse her hair as a delicious sigh escaped her lips, at the same time as his.

He shook his head to clear the erotic vision although it didn't help since his gaze kept going back to her. *God, I want—* He wasn't sure if he could put a name to his want at the moment.

With a deep breath, he moved his feet reluctantly to the cabinet under the sink so he could retrieve shampoo. He quickly escaped back out the door without wanting to return to fuck her against the wall with his aching cock.

The hotter the water, the better. The water sprayed out the head of the smaller shower. Lucky for him, one of his brothers had used the bathroom just a few days before when he'd had an accident out on the range and ended up in the middle of a wrestling match with a cow in the mud. There were still clean towels on the hook.

The water eased the ache between his shoulders as he sank back to let the liquid cascade over his back. Once he'd wet his hair, he quickly scrubbed the mud from the thick strands. After he'd shampooed his hair clean, he went to work on the dirt clinging to his arms and legs, but his sensitive cock wouldn't let the image of Peyton out of his brain. He would have to take care of the problem, otherwise there would be no denying what he wanted in the end.

He soaped up his hand before skimming the slick palm over his cock as he closed his eyes, losing himself in the dream of having her all to himself.

Those chocolate brown eyes of hers sparkled in the light as she swallowed his cock. The rough slide of her tongue along the shaft about drove him up on his toes. Lord, she knew how to give head.

"Close your eyes. Let me suck you off."

His affirmation came out in a high-pitched yes as she took him all the way to the back of her throat.

Oh shit. She has a tongue ring. The scrape of the metal ball on his cock drove him to the brink of exploding. When she cupped his balls in her hand and circled the head with her tongue, rasping the ball around and around, he lost it. Cum squirted out the end of his dick to coat her tongue as she swallowed every drop with reverence.

Jason slumped against the wall of the shower as he tried to catch his breath. He didn't think he'd ever come so hard in his life. *God help me when we finally have sex.*

When he finally was able to stand on legs that felt like noodles, he finished washing his body, then shut the shower off.

She would have to be done by now. He started to get hard again just thinking about her running around his home in nothing but a towel. A wicked little chuckle escaped his lips as he wrapped the towel around his waist before he opened the door.

The first thing he saw when he got to the living room took his breath away. She stood in nothing but one of his shirts. It had to be the sexiest thing he'd ever seen in his life. She had the sleeves rolled up to her elbows and the shirttails hung to mid-thigh. He almost swallowed his tongue.

"I hope you don't mind. I didn't have anything to put on, so I grabbed a shirt from your closest."

After he cleared his throat, he said, "Not at all. I'm glad you found something to wear."

She glanced down as she picked at the hem of the shirt. "It was the first thing I found."

"You couldn't be more sexier right now if you tried, darlin'."

He could tell by the reaction on her face he must have worn a little smirk on his lips. Her perfectly shaped eyebrow shot up over her left eye as her lips twitched when she tried not to smile.

"How long before the clothes are done?"

"Probably another fifteen minutes in the washer and at least thirty minutes in the dryer."

"Hmm." She crossed her arms over her chest, hiking the hem of the shirt up even further. "So what are we going to do while we wait for the clothes?"

"Since we aren't going to have down and dirty sex, how about I show you the rest of the house? But, let me throw some jeans on first."

"Of course."

He disappeared into his room to throw something on to cover his erection even though she would notice right away as it strained against the front of his pants. A groan escaped his lips as he shoved his cock into his jeans before he zipped them up. The scream he trapped in his throat almost escaped as he caught a few hairs in the zipper, ripping them out by the roots. *Holy fuck!*

"Everything okay?"

"Yes." The word came out in a squeak.

"Are you sure? You don't sound very good."

"I'm fine. I'll be out in a second." *Sweet mother of God.* He bit his lip as he shoved the zipper back down. Sweat poured from his temples as he stifled the scream in his throat. *That's what I get for trying to go commando.* "Well sex might not happen tonight." He pushed the jeans off his thighs and feet, grabbed a pair of boxers to slip on before he pulled his jeans back up over his hips. He wiped the sweat from his forehead with the back of his forearm as he blew out a long breath. *Good Lord that hurt.*

When he opened the door to the bedroom, she stood leaning against the opposite wall. "Are you sure you're okay? I thought I heard you scream."

"Nope. I'm fine." He walked out, shutting the door behind him.

"You're walking funny."

"Okay. All right. I caught my pubic hairs in my zipper."

He figured she'd laugh, but the gut rolling belly laughter escaping her mouth as she doubled over at the waist, made him frown. It wasn't that damned funny, was it?

"You…you got…caught in your zipper?"

"Yes."

"Oh God." She exploded in another round of laughter.

"It isn't funny."

"I'm-I'm sorry." She giggled. "Really, I'm sorry. I've caught pubic hair in zippers before, but—She exploded in laughter again as she reached out her hand. "Want me to kiss it and make it better?"

"Don't—don't touch it."

"I don't mean to laugh, but shit, that's funny."

"Are you done?" he asked, crossing his arms over his chest.

She pressed her lips together as her eyes danced with mirth. "Yes."

"Do you want to see the house or not?"

"Yes, I do.

He took her hand and led her back toward the front of the house. "The kitchen will be over there. I've got a few cabinets in, but the rest will be installed in the next coming weeks."

"I like them. Very nice." She stepped closer to the cabinets and ran her hands over the finish. "Did you buy them?"

"No. I made them myself."

"Wow. These are beautiful, Jason."

"Thanks." He pointed to the empty area where the stove stood, the dishwasher would go, and explained how he planned to put in granite countertops on them as soon as he had everything installed.

"Sounds like a beautiful kitchen anyone would be proud to cook in. Do you do a lot of cooking?"

"Actually, yeah. I do a lot of my own. We can eat with the family at the main house, but I spend as much time out here as I can. I like my space. After growing up with nine brothers, I like being alone. With three of them paired up now, there are even more at the table these days."

"I can totally see you standing at the stove making grilled cheese sandwiches for your kids."

"Kids?"

"You want kids someday, don't you? You know." She spun around. "Carry on the Young name."

"Maybe, but I sure ain't ready for kids right now. I still have some oats to sow."

"Oh, I'm sure you do. I've seen the women you come in with or pick up at the bar. I'm not blind."

"You've been watchin'?"

"I watch everything. I see a lot behind that bit of mahogany."

"I bet you do."

She scraped a fingernail down his chest, igniting his libido again even though his cock still ached from his brush with the zipper. "You really should be more careful about who you pick up at the bar."

"Why?"

"You know Tammy Ritz?" she asked, circling his nipple with a fingernail.

"Yeah. I went out with her a few weeks ago."

She shrugged before she walked toward the couch to take a seat. With her feet tucked under her, she said, "She's only after your name."

"How do you know this?"

"I heard her talking to her friends at one of the tables the other night. She thinks she's got you on the tow line, honey, and she plans to rein you in."

"Ain't happenin'." He took a seat on the opposite end of the couch, turning to face her.

"You'd better inform her of that little fact when you see her next."

"Oh I plan to. Thanks for the information."

"You're welcome. We can't have your magnificent body off the market so soon, now can we?"

"You're trying my self-control, lady."

"I hope so."

"Why are you hellfire bent on having me fuck you tonight?"

She turned to face him on the couch as she inched up the hem of the shirt she wore. She had nothing on under it. "I'm horny as hell and I'm sitting with a gorgeous male specimen. Why wouldn't I?"

His body went on high alert. She definitely kept putting that beautiful body out there, he might have to give in. He could only handle so much.

The washer beep as the load finished. Using it as an escape, he jumped to his feet to throw everything in the dryer. Maybe he could convince her to do something else like play pool. While he tossed the clothes in, he said, "How about a game of pool?"

"Sure." The closeness of her voice made him jump. He hadn't heard her come up behind him.

He swallowed hard as her warm breath caressed the back of his neck. She wasn't a small woman by any means if her mouth reached his neck. At over six feet, he liked his women tall. He liked her, everything about her on a physical level anyway. He didn't know much about her on a personal level, but he wasn't too interested in taking things beyond a physical relationship, so what did it matter.

"Great. Let me get these going and we'll go upstairs to what will be my game room. The walls aren't in, but the pool table is available for use." *Oh shit. That didn't come out right.* "I mean for us to play on." *I should just keep my mouth shut before I make this worse.*

"Anything you want, Jason, remember that."

She turned and walked out of the laundry room, giving him a little breathing space. It didn't help as the scent of her skin and his shampoo mixed in an intoxicating mingling of smells meant to drive him insane.

Good God, I need a cold shower now.

He stopped for a minute, bracing his hands on the tumbling dryer, but all it brought to mind was fucking her on the spinning washer.

"Jason? I thought we were going to play?"

"Fuck." He blew out a long breath, hoping it would calm his raging hard-on. It did nothing. "I'll be right there. You go on up." Oh, he wanted to play all right. Play with her gorgeous pussy all night long. He'd gotten a glimpse of the pink flesh when she'd hiked up the shirt, tempting him to throw everything to the wind and fuck her until they both couldn't breathe. Why did he torture himself this way? Why didn't he just give her what she so obviously wanted? He wasn't sure anymore. What difference would it make if he took care of her now or waited?

"Anticipation would make things so much sweeter."

Oh yeah, but...

"Leave it be."

Shit.

He turned to head up to the game room anticipating the torturous evening ahead of him until he could get her back into her clothes and on her way home. Why the hell he ever suggested washing her clothes for her, he wasn't sure. All he managed to do was afflict himself with the worse night in the history of Jason Young's life.

* * * *

Driving Jason insane with lust sounded like a great plan to Peyton. She'd wanted his body for some time and being this close was driving her insane. Her pussy throbbed with need, her clit swelling beyond the size comfortable to walk. She wanted him badly.

"Jason?"

"I'm coming." He cussed a blue streak quietly even though she could still hear him. "I mean I'll be right there."

She smiled to herself. She had him right where she wanted him. In so much pain, he'd give into her sooner or later. A little more teasing wouldn't hurt. She tapped her fingers against her lips. Maybe loosening a few buttons down the front of her shirt would push a few more of his buttons. A wicked giggle escaped from her mouth. *Oh this is fun.*

His steps on the stairs echoed in the empty room where she stood next to the nice sized pool table. *Leave it to a man to not have the walls up, but the pool table in place.*

"Ready?"

"Ready as I'll ever be," she replied, as she glanced down at the crotch of his jeans, noting the tented front. She had him right where she wanted him.

As he grabbed two pool cues from the corner, she unbuttoned two of the small pearl buttons on the front of the shirt she wore.

His eyes narrowed when he turned around and his gaze went to her chest. "Warm?"

"Yeah a little." She didn't think she'd fooled him one bit.

"I'll let you break."

Oh hell yeah. She took the cue as he moved to the table to rack. "I'm not very good at this."

"At what?" he asked, shoving the balls into the plastic triangle on the table.

"Playing pool."

"I'll teach you."

"Aren't you sweet?" The sugar sweetness in her voice didn't have him fooled as his eyes narrowed again while his hands grew still.

"Behave yourself, woman."

"I am. I'm not doing anything."

"I've got your number, darlin'. We already agreed not to have sex tonight."

"We did?"

"Okay, I said we weren't havin' sex tonight. I meant it."

"Of course, Jason." She lowered her gaze before she glanced up at him through her lashes. With a little luck, the coy look would work.

"Stop it, Peyton."

"Stop what?"

"The come-on. I don't want to have sex with you."

She glanced at the front of his jeans. "Are you sure?"

"All right. My cock wants to have sex with you, but my head says no. I'm listening to this," he tapped at his forehead, "head and not the one between my legs."

As she rolled her eyes, she said, "Fine. I'm doing everything in my power to seduce you, but apparently you aren't interested or have this manly sense of right and wrong that seems to be getting in the way. So be it."

"Do you know how to break?"

"Yes." She leaned over the table, giving him ample view of her naked ass. *Take that, stud.*

He groaned.

She smiled as she shoved the stick against the cue ball, shattering the perfect formation he placed at the other end of the table.

"Why do I get the feeling I've been shafted?"

"It was your idea to play." She moved around the table, shooting at intervals as she quickly cleared the table of all the solid colored balls.

The dryer beeped and she heard a long sigh with a *thank God* behind it.

She almost laughed out loud when he ran for the stairs, taking them two at a time down in his rush to get her clothes. Within seconds, he stood in front of her again, holding them out like they were on fire. "Here."

"Thanks." She proceeded to unbutton the shirt ever so slowly, just on the off chance she could tease him a little more before they parted ways for the night. If she had to be ready to explode, she was going to make damned sure he suffered just as much. After all, the man hadn't even kissed her.

"Peyton," he growled.

"Yes?"

"Take the damned clothes." He shoved the clothes at her before he spun on his heels, racing for the stairs again as she laughed behind him.

After several minutes, she shrugged and proceeded to get dressed. There would be another time to torture and fuck the gorgeous Jason Young before the summer concluded. Fuck him she would. Sooner or later, she'd have him in her bed spread eagle so she could ride his hips into tomorrow just to see if he was as good as the rumor mill proclaimed.

Chapter Three

Peyton no sooner got downstairs to find him completely dressed tapping his booted foot in a rapid tempo against the file floor near the front door. "Problem?"

"No. Let's go."

"Where are we going?" she asked, slipping on her muddy boots.

"To the bonfire."

"Why?"

"Because I can't be alone with you anymore tonight without giving into this thing between us."

"Thing?"

"Aren't you just full of questions?" He took her elbow, ushering her out to the truck with a firm hand.

"I didn't realize it was a problem, Jason. I mean, usually you are all over a willing woman, right?"

"Usually, yes, but not tonight."

"What is it? You won't take advantage of me?" She yanked her arm out of his grasp. "I mean really. I am free, white, and over twenty-one. I'm willing. I'm eager to sample what you have to offer. What's the deal?"

"That's right. I'm not taking advantage of you."

"If you don't want to fuck me, then just say it. I can find someone else to ease the ache, cowboy."

He dragged her into his embrace with a hand on both of her upper arms until her breasts were squashed against the hard plains of his chest. "Let's get one thing straight, babe. I'm gonna fuck you sooner or later, but not tonight. It's not the right time for us and that's all I'm sayin'."

As she drew in a breath to tell him where to take his right time, he slammed his mouth down on hers in a lip crushing kiss meant to melt any resistance she might have. Not that she would resist at all. This is what she wanted from the moment she locked gazes with this gorgeous hunk of manflesh.

She softened her lips until they molded to the hard line of his. He growled low in his throat as he wrapped his arms around her back and pulled her in tighter. When she brushed her tongue against the seam of his lips, he lost control, bruising her lips to deepen the kiss even further.

He finally pulled back far enough she could see the glittering of his blue eyes in the moonlight overhead. "Don't push me, babe."

"Why not, stud? I can handle you."

"Right now, you wouldn't be able to. I'm horny enough to break you in half."

"I can take it." The tip of her fingernail skipped over the buttons as she raked it down his chest. "Let's stay here and fuck like bunnies."

"You don't understand."

"I want you."

"I know."

"Then why not?"

"Peyton, please don't push this."

She sighed and stepped out of his embrace. "Fine. Let's go the bonfire."

The physical relaxing of his shoulders told her he was relieved she'd backed off. Oh, she understood all right, probably more than he knew. He didn't want her. That's fine, she guessed, even though disappointment raced through her. She'd never had a man turn her down before. Didn't they all want sex whenever or wherever they could get it? A man like Jason Young didn't turn down anyone she'd ever seen when she'd had the chance to observe him at the bar. He *always* went home with someone. What was it about her that turned him off? The piercings? The tats? Well to hell with him then. She couldn't do anything about those things if they were a problem for him. If he didn't like them, then so be it. They were a part of her, part of her personality. Maybe he didn't like them on his woman even though he had tats himself? She shrugged as she grabbed the door to his truck to open it and haul herself inside. She'd ride this pony as far as it would go, then move on with her life. There were other fish in the sea and plenty of men to choose from.

Without another word between them, they drove back to the main ranch house where she could see the roaring fire licking at the sky with the bright orange flames. Such a cowboy thing, a bonfire. Well maybe not, she did like camping out and sitting by a fire cuddling with some guy. Not that she'd done it in a long time, but it was still nice to sit under the blanket of an inky sky with stars twinkling above. Someday, she'd get the chance to spread out a soft quilt in the back of a pickup, lay her head on a guy's chest and stare at the sky for hours. Why had her daydreams always seemed to revolve around Jason lately, she wasn't sure, but she needed to put it behind her. He apparently wasn't attracted to her that way.

Maybe he liked men?

Nah, that was stupid. His prowess with the women of Bandera bordered on legendary.

So why wasn't he interested in her?

She shrugged. Oh well. Time to move on.

As soon as he parked the truck, she jumped out and slammed the door behind her. No more waiting on or dreaming of Jason Young. He was part of the past now.

"Hey Peyton!" Jonathan shouted, coming to his feet from his spot at the fire. "You got cleaned up easy enough."

"Yeah."

Jonathan glanced at her, then back to Jason. "Oh. I see."

The dejected look on his face gave her an idea. Jonathan seemed like a nice enough guy, maybe a little shy and nerdy, but what the hell. Jason didn't want her. That stung her pride a little. Maybe one of the other Young brothers might quell the itch she had before the night concluded. She moved right to his side and sat down. "Sit with me."

"Uh, okay." He swiped his palms down the leg of his jeans before he took a seat next to her, glancing quickly at his brother.

Jason frowned, but didn't say a word as he took a seat opposite them across the fire.

"So what do you do around the ranch, Jonathan? I don't see you in The Dusty Boot like your brothers very often."

"I'm not much of a drinker."

"You don't have to drink to come to the bar. There are pool tables, dancing, darts, all kinds of things to do not involving alcohol."

"True, but I'm not real comfortable in bars. I like spending time with the website and marketing for the ranch. It keeps me busy most days."

"Do you do the cowboy stuff much?"

"Not really. I leave that to my brothers." He shifted so his hips weren't quite touching hers anymore. "I ride. You can't grow up on a ranch and not ride, but I'm not as comfortable on a horse or herding cattle as my brothers are. I mean look at Jason? He's all about the cowboy stuff. He wants to breed bulls for the PBR."

"PBR?"

"Professional Bull Riders Association." He smiled down at her. "You don't do cowboy much, do you?"

"No." She laughed. "Is it so apparent I'm lacking in the Texas pastime?"

"Yeah, a little. Do you know anything about a cattle ranch?"

"Not really. Why don't you teach me," she said, looping her hand through the crook of his arm. "I'm eager to learn." She glanced across the fire and noticing Jason's eyes narrowed, their gazes locked in a battle of wills.

"Well, we run longhorns on our property. They are one of the original cattle to be raised here in the Texas Hill Country. They are a hearty breed of cattle who do well here where the land isn't so grassy and plentiful. Our ranch is pretty big for one out here where several of the local ranches are selling off to developers. Jeff has been very adamant about us not selling off any of our property to them. Keep everything in the family, you know."

"Is Jeff like the foreman?"

"Yeah, pretty much. He's tight reined on what goes on around here although he's mellowed out a lot since Terri came along."

"Didn't she just have a baby?"

"Yeah, not too long ago." He shifted on his seat. "We also have guests we rent out rooms and cabin space to, especially in the summer months. They come from all over to learn about cattle ranching, I guess. I'm not quite sure what the fascination with it is, but they pay to come. It's a great income for the ranch when selling cattle isn't paying so much."

"How fascinating."

Jonathan's voice faded as he went on to talk about the website building for the ranch. Not like she wasn't interested, but the glare she was receiving from Jason had shivers rolling down her back. *Why does he have to affect me this way? Damn cowboy.*

"So that's what I do all day," Jonathan finished.

"Wow. Sounds like you really stay busy."

"I try. There's a lot to do when you are marketing a guest ranch plus managing the website for both the cattle ranch and the guest ranch. We have two websites. One for buyers of the cattle and one for guests of the ranch."

"Care to take a walk with me?"

"Uh, sure. I can show you the front of the main lodge. It's pretty cool all lit up with the lights."

"Awesome." She rose to her feet, not relinquishing her hold on his arm as they headed for the front part of the ranch. The tingling along her back let her know Jason's gaze followed their every move, making her wonder whether he would come after her.

As they rounded the house toward the front, she caught a glimpse of someone sitting in one of the rocking chairs, but the moment she turned her head to ask Jonathan about the man, the figure on the porch had disappeared. *Weird.*

"We have the rocking chairs out here for people to sit so they can enjoy the sunrise or evening air. It's really cool out here in the early mornings."

"Are you an early riser?"

"Yeah, most of the time I'm out here by myself with a cup of coffee before anyone else is even up. Joey and Jeff are up with the sun most mornings too, dealing with the ranch stuff."

"I bet the cowboy life tends to do that to you. Does Jason get up early too?" *Damn, Peyton! Just shut up about him.* "Never mind. None of my business."

"Are you two having a fight or somethin'."

"No, why?"

"Well, you left with him earlier and came to the bonfire with him." He pulled her hand out from around his arm. "I don't mess with my brother's girl."

"I'm not his girl."

"Then why did you leave with him?"

"He offered to wash my clothes after I got in the mud."

"You were naked at his house?"

Well, fuck a duck. She stepped from his side to take a seat on one of the rockers. "Yeah, I guess you could say that, although I wore one of his shirts the whole time my clothes were in his washer."

"Listen, Peyton. You're a really nice girl and I think you're hot, but I won't come between the two of you."

"There isn't anything between me and Jason, Jonathan. Trust me. He doesn't want me."

"I can't see why not. You're beautiful."

"Thanks, but apparently he doesn't think so. I mean he could have had me any time he wanted me, but he won't. I don't know what to think."

Jason's voice penetrated the darkness as he came around the corner. "Jonathan."

"Jason."

"Peyton."

"Jason. What do you want?"

"Nothin'. I wanted to make sure everything was okay."

"Everything is fine. I'm having a great conversation with your brother."

"It's not what it looks like, Jase."

"It doesn't matter, Jonathan. There isn't anything going on between me and Peyton anyway."

Just as I thought.

"I won't step on toes, Jason, you know that."

"No toes here, buddy." Jason clapped Jonathan on the shoulder. "Go for it."

Bastard. "Thanks for giving him permission to pursue me, you asswipe!"

"What?"

She stood up, bringing her five-foot-nine-inch frame as close to Jason as possible. Intimidation wasn't her strong point, but rage at his audacity washed through her now. "Just because you don't want me, doesn't mean other men don't. I can get a guy if I want one whether you think so or not. I don't need your fucking permission to date someone. There are plenty of men out there."

They stood nose to nose.

"I didn't say you couldn't. I just didn't want there to be any mistake that we were a couple."

"We aren't."

"No, we aren't."

"Then leave me the fuck alone. If I want to date Jonathan, then I will."

"Go ahead."

"Fine!" She turned around only to find Jonathan had melted into the darkness leaving her alone with Jason...again.

* * * *

"What an absolutely infuriating female you are!" He took two steps back and raked his fingers through his hair. He'd never understand women at this rate. "Why can't you leave well enough alone?"

"I wasn't doing a damned thing but talking to your brother."

"He's not your type."

"What the hell do you know!"

"I know you."

"You don't know shit about me."

"You're independent, hard-headed, impossible, stubborn," his voice dropped an octave, "sexy, gorgeous, and hot."

He watched her breath catch in her throat. What the hell was he getting at? He didn't want her, right?

"Leave it be, Jason. You don't want me, remember?"

"I never said that, you did."

"Then why push me away?"

"Because I don't want you..."

"See?"

He grabbed her arm, dragging her back until her breasts brushed his chest. Her nipples puckered at the friction.

"Let me finish." With her lips pressed together, she tempted him beyond reason. He wanted her in the worst way. "I want you between my sheets. Me between your legs eating you until you come all over my face. I want my dick buried so deep in your pussy, you scream my name loud enough to disturb the cattle. My cock aches for the warmth of you wrapped around it."

"Then why?" she asked, her voice barely a whisper.

"You're different."

"Different?"

"I don't know how to explain it. There is something about you. I don't want to just fuck your brains out and walk away the next morning like I've done so many times before. You aren't like all the other women in Bandera. You don't wear cowboy boots. You have a tongue ring, which by the way is hot as hell. You have a tat on your breast." He skimmed his index finger over the swell of her breast where the tattoo sat below her shirt. "I want to explore you way beyond just a quick fuck."

She pushed out of his arms, rubbing her skin like she was cold. "I'm not looking for a relationship, Jason."

"I know you aren't. I don't think I am either, but…"

"But?"

"I wish I knew. I don't want to hurt you, Peyton. I'm afraid if we just fuck, then you'll be hurt by whatever is between us."

"I'm willing to take the chance."

"I'm not sure I am."

"What are you afraid of?"

"You." He'd just bared his soul to the one woman who might be able to crush him and he didn't care. Okay, well a little, but what did it mean? He wasn't supposed to think of any woman as much as he thought about her over the last few months. Every time he'd been at the bar, there she was with her long hair either back in a braid or cascading down her shoulders like it was now. The itch to wrap his hand in those strands and tug overwhelmed him at times. Some other thoughts had him running his fingers through it to feel the silky softness against his palms. She didn't seem to take to one type of man over another. He'd never seen her leave with anyone either. What did she like? What type of man did she go for? His type? He didn't know, but he wanted to find out.

"Why are you so afraid of me? I'm just a woman looking for a good time."

Crack. His resolve split wide open. He had a conversation with his reflection this morning about how he would stop using women for his own pleasure and here this one just threw a noodle into the soup. He exhaled sharply, recalling the conversation he had with his mother about this very thing. Nina was all over him about his playboy ways. *But, I'm only in my twenties. I shouldn't be thinking of settling down with one woman, right?*

Peyton laughed, drawing him out of his reverence. "Don't sound so relieved, Jason. I told you before I'm not in for a relationship right now, just to relieve a little pressure between the thighs if you're willin'."

"I'm willin'."

"Then shall we go back to your place to heat up some sheets?" she asked, running her tongue around the shell of his ear.

His cock jumped behind the fly of his jeans. It seemed like he'd been forever horny around her, but tonight would see the end of his self-induced torture…he hoped.

Chapter Four

The truck no more stopped at the front of the house and they were both out of the vehicle locked in an embrace. They stumbled together toward the front door, his mouth on hers, doing his best to get her clothes off in the process. A shirt here, another there. Nothing mattered but getting him naked and between her thighs.

She ached for this man.

The calluses on his palm abraded her nipple into a tortured point as Jason walked her backward down the hall from the front room to his bedroom. His mouth never left hers. Their tongues tangled as they explored in a way she hadn't before. *I think he plans to devour me.*

He lifted his head when they reached the door to his room and he backed her against the expanse. "I hope you plan on spending the entire night because it's going to take me that long to find all your hot spots."

"If you want me to."

"Oh yeah. I plan on fucking you every which way but up."

"I can't wait."

He turned the knob on the door as his mouth dove for hers again. He flipped the light on only seconds before he scooped her up and deposited her onto the bed, then followed her to the mattress. Somewhere along the path to the bedroom, he'd lost his shirt. The hair on his chest tickled against her breasts as she moaned into his mouth. She wanted him so badly, she could feel the wetness between her legs. This kind of thing didn't happen with a man or hadn't before. It normally took her a bit to get going, but not with Jason. *Figures.*

"I can smell you," he whispered against her neck before raking his teeth along the curve of her throat.

Shivers danced along her arms and legs. The weight of his body on hers felt right, so right. The warmth of his skin singed her body with a delicious heat all its own. She wrapped her jean clad legs around his hips, urging him on with a raise of her pelvis. Need had her in its claws, ripping at her sanity a little at a time.

His lips skimmed over the slope of her shoulder on their journey to her breast. A gasp escaped her mouth the moment he closed over the tip. Desire exploded through her, soaking her panties in preparation for him.

He lifted his head momentarily as the soft whisper of breath pulled the taut bud into an achy point. "Can you come from nipple play?"

"I don't know. "

"Let's try, shall we?"

For a solid ten minutes, he sucked, pulled, pinched, bit and tortured her nipples until she thought she would go mad. They were sensitive, yes, but she'd never had a man focus solely on tormenting them until she thought she would lose her mind. Jason did. Her belly clenched as he nipped at the tip with his teeth. *God, I might actually be able to orgasm from this.*

He released her breast much to her dismay, but when his hands worked at the button near her waist, she lifted her hips so he could get her jeans off. A wicked grin spread across his mouth as he tossed one boot, then the other before he whipped the pants down and off in one tug.

When his lips returned to nip at the achy peak of her left breast, his finger did a slow crawl from her knee, up her thigh, across the mound of pubic hair to glance off her clit. She exploded into a body numbing orgasmic kaleidoscope of colors behind her closed eyelids. "Jason!"

He lifted his head, revealing the smug grin on his face. "There it is. I knew you could do it."

Her breath came out in a halting seesaw of air as she tried to bring her heart rate back to normal. "That was…"

"Awesome?"

"Amazing. Do it again."

One eyebrow rose over his eye like he couldn't believe she asked that. Honestly, she couldn't believe she asked it of him. She wasn't a demanding lover. Normally things were all about pleasing the guy, right? Wasn't it supposed to be all about the guy? Half the time, she'd be lucky to even orgasm once when she had sex. "I mean, if you want to that is."

"Oh, I want and you'll get, babe. No doubt. It turns me on somethin' fierce to watch you come."

"Really?"

"What the hell kind of men have you been with?"

She shrugged as she tried to close her legs, but his body had her trapped open and ready for him. "I don't know. I don't get a lot out of it sometimes."

His hand moved between her legs, scooping up her cum on his fingers before he spread it around her clit. "Not with me, darlin'. I take care of my women."

Women. That's not what I want to hear. "I'm sure you do, cowboy."

"You'll see. You'll be walkin' funny tomorrow if I have anything to say about it and in my house, I do."

He slid down her body, kissing his way from her breasts, across her belly, and down between her thighs.

Her breath caught in her throat as his mouth hovered over her pussy. The first swipe of his tongue had her hips coming off the bed as a groan escaped her lips. There wasn't anything better than a starving man feasting on her pussy. Not that she'd had it very often, but she loved it when they did this. "Oh God, please, Jason, don't stop."

"I don't plan to until you come all over my face."

The rough pad of his tongue drove her desire higher. Each swipe and each lick had her hips meeting his face as she lifted her pelvis. He laid one arm across her hips to keep her down. With her fingers tangled in his hair, she rode out the sensations to the peak of fulfillment as she screamed his name again at the top of her lungs.

"We can try for a little louder, darlin'. I don't think they heard you at the main lodge."

"Bastard," she gasped, panting hard. The nerves down there jumped in an erratic rhythm as she came down from her high. "Now you."

"I'm good. I'll be nice and snug in your warm place here in a minute."

"But I should give you head or something."

"You don't have to."

"Seriously? I thought all guys liked getting head?"

"I'm not saying I don't like it or I don't want it, but tonight is about you and your needs. I want to make sure you never forget tonight."

"Oh I won't," she whispered, taking his face between her hands to bring his mouth to hers. "I've been waiting for this for a long time."

He kissed her slow, long and deep, meshing their mouths together like they'd done this a thousand times before. Maybe they had in another life. The thought of it made her mind spin out of control.

"Mmm. Hang on. I need to get a condom out of my wallet."

"Okay."

He moved off her to remove his boot and pants. When his cock sprang free, she sighed in appreciation. He really was built in all the right places, long, heavily muscled legs, trim hips, flat, washboard abs, muscular chest with just a bit of dark chest hair, and kissable lips. When he bent over to retrieve his wallet from the back pocket of his pants, she got a nice view of his taut ass. *Holy shit! No wonder it looks so nice in Wranglers.*

"Appreciatin' the view?"

"Oh yeah. You have a nice ass."

"Why thank you, ma'am."

"Don't call me ma'am. You're older than I am."

"Why? It's a term of endearment."

"For your mother or grandmother maybe."

"No. It's a sign of respect from any cowboy to a woman. Haven't you had anyone call you ma'am before?"

"Yeah, but it's usually at work when they open the door for me."

"Well then, there you go."

"Call me darlin'."

"You like that do you?" he asked, his eyes glittering in the lamplight as he cocked his head to the side.

"Yes. There is somethin' about a cowboy calling me darlin'."

"I'll do it any time you want, darlin'."

She shivered as he rolled the condom over his erection before he slowly came toward her in a deliberate, almost panther like saunter. *Damn, he is what wet dreams are made of, at least mine anyway.* "Fuck me, Jason."

"My pleasure, darlin'."

He moved between her thighs, settling himself in the cradle of her pelvis. The moment he slid his cock slowly between her pussy lips, she thought she'd died and gone to heaven. With his cock slowly being pushed inside her, she gasped at the first moment of penetration. A soft moan escaped with each inch. He fit perfectly.

When he was completely inside her, she sighed with the fullness and rightness of having him there. "You feel good."

"Oh, babe, you have no idea how good you feel. Warm, wet, just right."

As he started to move his hips, she wound her legs around behind him. He slowly moved inside her, driving her mad with want as he painstakingly brought her to the brink of insanity again before he would let her fall over. She'd fool him though. She doubted she could come again after having two orgasms already, but he could try—and lord help her, she wanted him to with everything inside her.

"You'll have another before I'm through."

"I can't."

His hand slid down between them. "You will."

"Jason."

"Peyton."

"Do it hard."

"Oh yeah." With a snap of his hips, he drove his cock deep inside her.

Her stomach clenched as he hit her G spot with each thrust. She didn't think she'd ever had a G spot orgasm, but she just might tonight.

His pace increased until he was slamming his cock inside her so hard, she had to brace herself on his headboard to keep from banging her head. "Yes, yes, yes."

She felt his finger on her clit, rubbing first one side and then the other before he took the wetness seeping between them and spread it around the tip. She thought her head would blow off as her body exploded in a mind-numbing orgasm that left her shaking each time he shoved his cock inside her again.

"Oh God," he whispered as he came to a shuddering halt. "Fuck yeah."

He collapsed on top of her with his face resting in the crook of her neck. She smoothed her hands down his sweaty back as their bodies pulsed and shivered together until their hearts stopped galloping out of their chests. He'd just given her the best sex of her life.

Chapter Five

Her fingertips felt soft against his back as he allowed himself the comfort of her arms. He didn't usually do this, cuddle thing with women after they had sex, but with Peyton, it felt right.

"That was somethin', cowboy."

"I'm glad you enjoyed yourself."

"Oh definitely." She grunted. "But you need to get off my chest so I can breathe. You're kind of heavy."

He laughed as he rolled to her side. "Better?"

She gasped a few breaths. "Yeah."

"Sorry."

"No problem. I'm just not used to a couple hundred pounds of manflesh on my chest."

With his finger, he tucked a strand of stray hair behind her ear before he kissed her nose. "You were fantastic."

"Thanks."

"Are you not used to having orgasms or somethin'?"

"Why do you say that?"

"Because you acted like having three was out of the question."

"I've never had three with a guy before. Half the time, I'm lucky to get one."

"You're with the wrong man then, darlin'."

"Apparently so." She skimmed her hand down his chest. "I think you're the right man."

"For now."

"Yeah, for now."

He swung his legs over the side of the bed and sat up. "Do you want something to drink? I'm kind of parched after all the exercise."

"I could use some water, if you have some."

"Bottled or tap?"

"Either is fine. I'm assuming you are on well water?"

"Yep. Best water in the territory right here on Young property."

She pushed herself up on the bed and shoved a couple of strands of hair off her forehead. "Tap is fine then."

He stopped to stare for a minute thinking she had to be the prettiest thing he'd ever seen in his bed. Of course, he hadn't had anyone in this bed before now, but she was a great first.

"What?"

"Nothing. Why?"

"You're staring." She smiled as her cheeks turned a slight shade of pink.

"You're beautiful."

She crossed her arms over her chest to hide her breasts. "No I'm not."

"Yes, you are." He shook his head to clear his thoughts. "I'll be right back." A pair of old sweat shorts sat on the floor, so he grabbed them, disposed of the condom in the trash before he pulled the pants on and went out the door toward the kitchen. No use getting all gooey over her. She already said she didn't want anything to happen beyond tonight. Things had been hotter than the Fourth of July between them though. He hadn't come so hard in his life until this moment with her. What made her so special? Yeah, she's pretty, got a great set of knockers, killer ass, and lips a man would die to have wrapped around his cock, but other than that?

"Isn't that enough?"

Well maybe, but I don't want anything permanent either.

Once he reached the kitchen, he grabbed a soda from the refrigerator and a glass for some water from the cabinet. As he filled the glass, he glanced out the window. He could see the glow of the lights from the main lodge house in the distance. He loved his family, but he was glad he built his place far enough away so he could have his own privacy. Now if he could just finish the house, he might actually think about settling down. The thought startled him. Never in a million years would the thought cross his mind any other time. Why tonight? Why after he made love to Peyton? He shook his head. No, he fucked her. Plain and simple. He didn't make love to any woman.

"Jason? Everything okay?"

"Yeah. I'll be right there." He shook his head as he headed back into the bedroom. He had a waiting, willing woman in his bed for the night. He would think about the rest later.

When he walked back into the bedroom, he found the most amazing sight. Peyton lay on his pillow with her hair fanned out like a cloud around her head, her legs spread apart and her fingers working her clit.

"I started without you."

"Holy shit, woman, that's hot."

"What? Never seen a woman pleasure herself before?"

"It doesn't matter if I have or not, I've never seen you do it. That is about the sexiest thing I've ever seen."

"I want you again."

"Fuck yeah."

"Are you up for an all-night rodeo, handsome?"

"More than up for it." He watched her gaze drop to the front of his shorts as they tented from his erection standing straight and hard against his abdomen.

"I see." She gave him a come-hither look as she continued to pleasure herself. "If you don't hurry, I might come all by myself."

"I'd like to see that."

"Would you now?"

"Uh-huh."

"Sorry, cowboy. After you made me climax three times, I think it'll take a little more stimulation to get me there again."

"Is that a challenge?"

"Only if you want it to be."

"You're on, babe." He handed her the glass of water and took a sip from the can in his hand. "Drink up. You'll need to stay hydrated if we plan on ridin' until mornin'."

"Will you take me home?"

"What? Now?"

She laughed. "No, in the morning."

"Of course, I will. I never push my women out of my bed until they're ready to leave."

"There it is again." A frown marred her pretty face as her lips thinned into an aggravated line.

"What?"

"Your women. Can we not discuss the women before me? Not that I have any foolhardy notion that there weren't hundreds before me and will be hundreds after me, but I really don't like hearing about them."

"Sorry."

"Thank you." She finished her water before setting the glass on the nightstand. "Now, where were we?" She raked her fingernails down his chest. "Oh yeah, right about here." His shorts dropped to the floor as she took his cock in her palm.

Fuck yeah.

His cock swelled even more when she opened her mouth and took the head between her full lips. *Good God.* He thought he would die right there. His legs shook. His cock ached. His balls felt like they would implode. When she moved one hand down between his legs, he though his head would spin around. "Oh God." The slide of her tongue ring on the underside of his cock drove him wild.

She hummed deep in her throat as she took the rest of his cock into her mouth. His legs almost buckled as his breath lodged in his chest. He cupped her head between his palms, threading his fingers through the thick strands of her gorgeous hair. He wanted to wrap a hand in those brown strands and pull so badly, he ached with it.

"Mmm."

Fuck, he was about to lose it down her throat if she didn't stop and he didn't want to come that way. He wanted the warmth of her pussy around him when he lost his load. "Peyton, stop."

She grabbed his ass cheeks in both hands, scooted closer and held on.

"I can't hold...*fuck!*" He exploded into her mouth, shooting his entire load of cum straight down her throat in a climax so violent, his whole body shook from the force. "Baby, I didn't want to come like that."

She wiped her face with the back of her hand. "I wanted you to. You don't taste half bad. A little salty, but overall, not bad."

After he sank down on the edge of the bed to catch his breath, he turned to smile at her. It had been a long time since a woman had sucked him off. Not as if he didn't like it when they did, but he usually took care of them, not the other way around. "Thank you."

"For what?"

"For sucking me off. You didn't have to."

"I know. I wanted to." She tilted her head to the side. "Don't tell me you've never had a woman suck you off before."

He pushed a strand of hair behind her ear. "That's not it at all, it's just I don't let them do it very often. I'm more interested in taking care of you rather than you take care of me."

With a shrug of her shoulders, she said, "Well I wanted to take care of you for a change. I'll get mine. I'm sure you'll take care of me."

"Most definitely." He reached over to caress her breast with his right hand. The full mound of flesh fit perfectly in his palm. "You have fantastic tits."

She laughed.

"What's so funny? I'm being serious here."

"Tits?"

"Oh. Sorry. Breasts."

"It doesn't bother me, but I think it's kind of funny to have them referred to as tits when you are in the middle of having sex unless it's rough and tumble sex."

"Do you want rough and tumble sex? I can accommodate, I'm sure."

"How about you fuck me against the wall?" she asked, glancing up at him through her lashes.

"I could since this room is about the only one in the house with walls."

"Sounds like fun."

"First you need prepped."

"Prepped?"

"Lie back and spread those gorgeous thighs for me."

"Oh, I can do that."

She leaned back on her elbows on the pillow with her legs open. Her pussy glistened with juices already wetting the pink surface. *Good God, in heaven.* She had a nice pussy, all plump and ready for his mouth. The smell of her arousal tempted him beyond endurance as he situated himself between her legs. His shoulders kept her thighs spread when he rubbed his whiskered cheek over the sensitive area. He swiped one finger down her slit, from her clit to her waiting opening. "You're so sexy."

"Taste me. I want your tongue," she whispered, watching when he inhaled her scent right before he went in for more of her taste.

She relaxed back against the pillows, her gaze never leaving his face. With both hands, she cupped her breasts, pinching the nipples as she rolled them between her fingers. Soft little moans escaped her mouth, fueling his already out of control libido.

Her engorged clit peeked out from beneath its hood, waiting for a nip of his teeth. He didn't disappoint. Her hips surged up as a hearty groan exploded from her mouth.

"Yes. More."

Juices flowed from her, coating his tongue and chin. *Such sweetness from a beautiful woman.*

He continued to lick, suck and nibble at her flesh until everything turned a bright red. She exploded in a bone shaking, body trembling orgasm.

"Fuck," she gasped that desperate, breathless sound only a satisfied woman can make.

"Now I'm going to pound into you so hard and so fast, you'll make those little mewing sounds I love so much."

"I don't mew."

"Wanna bet? You made them when I fucked you last time, but this time, it's going to happen with each thrust." He picked up her boneless body, wrapping her legs around his hips as he slid inside her hot, waiting warmth. With her clasping his cock so tight, he thought she might break it in half, he pushed her against the wall, pulled her legs up over his forearms and slammed into her.

"Ah, God."

"Oh yeah." The little mewling sounds escaped her mouth with each thrust, earning a smile from him. He knew she would. She was as responsive as a woman could get and he loved hearing the sounds coming from her mouth. "That's it, kitten. Come for me."

"I can't." A gasp escaped her lips.

"Yes you can, baby. Yes you can."

"Please."

"Please what, darlin'?"

"Harder. God, please harder."

He spread his legs to give himself a little more leverage. The change in angle had his balls drawing up against his groin in preparation for his own release. If he didn't clamp down on his orgasm, he'd come before her. That wasn't an option in his world.

The *slap, slap, slap* of wet flesh echoed in the room. The smell of sex drove his desire higher.

Her pussy clamped down on his cock as the flesh quivered. She was going to come if he had anything to say about it. If only he could reach her clit. "Reach down and finger yourself."

"What?" Her panting gasps resonated in his ear.

"Finger your clit. Make yourself come."

Her small hand snaked down between them until he could feel her fingers on her clit. Her breathing sped up. Her pussy creamed as she quickly moved her fingers around her clit.

"I'm gonna come."

"Yes."

She screamed his name just as he lost his own battle with holding his orgasm down. He couldn't stop the flow of cum from the end of his dick any more than he could stop the world of spinning. Liquid seeped down between them, coating his thighs.

"Ah fuck!"

* * * *

"What?"

"I forgot the condom." He slowly slid out of her, releasing her legs so she could stand on her own. "God, I'm such a fucking idiot!"

"Easy, slick. It'll be fine."

"No it won't. I never forget a condom unless I've been with a woman a while."

"I'm on birth control. It's fine."

He shoved his hand through his hair in a motion she'd come to realize meant he was agitated. "What about other things? I mean I'm clean."

"Me too." She leaned against the wall for support as her legs still shook from the force of her orgasm. Having so many so close together almost hurt, in a good way. "Not like I fuck around a lot, Jason."

"I didn't think you did, although I really don't know you very well."

"Yet you were willing to fuck my brains out?"

"It's not like that, Peyton. You and me are like two peas in a pod."

"How so?" she asked, moving on shaky legs toward the pile of clothes on the floor. The need to be covered overwhelmed her. Somehow, this wasn't the way she thought their conversation *afterward* should go. Not like she expected professions of love or anything, but she sure didn't think he would go all prude on her.

"We both want the same things. Sex without strings, right?"

"Yep." She slipped her underwear over her feet, and then stood to pull them up.

"What are you doing?"

"Getting dressed."

"Why? I thought you were staying the night?"

"I don't think that is such a good idea."

"I don't understand."

"This is just a fling, Jason, nothing more. I mean, not that I wouldn't mind having sex with you now and again. What happened here tonight proved we're pretty good together. I just don't want anyone to get any ideas we are a couple. If your family sees you taking me home in the morning, they might think there is more to this than there is."

"True."

"Good. Then why don't you put some clothes on so you can run me home." He frowned as he watched her pull her chemise on. "Problem?"

"No. I just like watching you."

"Get dressed?"

"Yeah. It's sexy."

She rolled her eyes as she smiled. Why did she think this guy was the most adorable cowboy she'd ever seen and there had been a few of them in the couple of years she's lived in Bandera. "Put some clothes on, cowboy, so we can go."

"Fine, but don't blame me if we stop somewhere along a back road and fuck again before we get to your place."

"I'm not havin' sex with you in your truck."

"Wanna bet?"

They were both laughing by the time they made it out the door. She really didn't think he'd fuck her on the way home, but sure enough, they stopped at a small gate outside his parents place. "What are you doing?"

"We're gonna fuck again before I get you home."

"Really, Jason. This behavior is so becoming of you. I love it!"

"Good." He pulled through the gate until he found a flat spot near a tree. "I have a couple of sleeping bags behind the seat. Let's fuck under the stars."

The minute he jumped out of the truck, she had to giggle. In all the time she'd been sexually active, she'd never had sex in the back of a pickup under the stars. This would be a first, although she kind of hoped there would be more firsts with him. He kind of turned her upside down and inside out with his kissable lips, luscious body and killer personality. She just hoped she wasn't getting in over her head with him. The last thing she needed to do was fall head over heels in love with a playboy like Jason Young.

Chapter Six

Morning raised its ugly head as Peyton rolled over in her bed. The night before had been what sexy dreams were made of and she didn't want to wake up from that particular dream quite yet. Sunlight poured through the lacy curtains on her window, willing her to open her eyes and face the day, a day without Jason Young next to her. She had the memories though. Those would have to do until the next time she could get him to make love to her like he had last night.

"You are so screwed, Peyton Matthews." She sat up as she pushed the hair out of her face. "The last thing you should be worrying about is getting that man back in your bed. You need to focus on school and work."

She had to work tonight at The Dusty Boot so she rolled back over on her bed and closed her eyes. She'd need the extra sleep if she was going to make it through her two a.m. shift without being tired to the bone.

Her cell jingled on the side of her bed, indicating a text message had come through. *Who could that be? The person obviously doesn't know I don't answer before noon.* She struggled to sit up, realizing again she was completely naked beneath the sheet. When Jason had finally got her home, she'd quickly stripped off her clothes and went to bed since it was three in the morning by then.

After she tucked the sheet around her breasts, she grabbed her phone to check the message.

Hey beautiful. Are you up?

"He seriously thinks he's talking to me at this time of morning?" she grumbled, as she stared at the screen. "He's too damned chipper for nine a.m." She huffed as she tried to decide whether to put the phone back on the nightstand or whether to actually answer his text. After a moment, she decided on the later.

I'm up barely. You're too damned high-spirited for this early. What the hell?

I'm always up early. I'm a cowboy, remember?

Yeah and I'm a bartender who has to work until two in the morning tonight. I planned on sleeping in today.

Sorry, babe. I wanted to say good morning.

Is that it?

Isn't that enough?

I suppose. Can I go back to sleep now?

LOL Sorry to wake you. Have a great day!

You too.

She laid the phone back on the nightstand before lying back on her soft, comfortable bed, and closing her eyes. Sleep wouldn't come. Flashes of memory bombarded her brain as she relived every touch and every caress from the night before. Her body caught fire. She needed to come…badly, but she couldn't. She hadn't been able to masturbate herself to completion in some time. Not since Charles broke down her self-esteem and made her feel like she wasn't the least bit sexy. Some of the piercings had come from his emotional abuse. She didn't cut, but she felt the need to pierce herself to take care of the heartbreak from him.

"God, I thought I was over this."

Tears burned the back of her eyes as she fought not to cry. Jason thought she was sexy, damn it, so why didn't she believe him. Maybe she needed to talk to him, but how? He didn't want to take this past a physical relationship. Neither did she, right? A man in her life would complicate things. School, life, work. She didn't have time for a man on a regular basis.

"Well sleep is out of the question. Maybe I should take a nice, hot shower and do some house cleaning. That always gets my mind on other things."

School would be starting soon and she needed to focus on that, but for now, she needed to get out of this funky frame of mind so she could start living again. The counselor she saw regularly helped her tremendously and that's why she decided to go into this particular line of work herself. Hopefully someday she would be able to help someone just like her.

She flipped the sheet off before she walked to her dresser to retrieve some clothes. A shower would be a good place to start her day. Maybe taking a nap later so she wouldn't be so damned tired tonight during her shift wouldn't be such a bad idea. "We'll see how things go."

For the next several hours, she cleaned to the tune of country music blaring in her earbuds. She liked different sounds so her music consisted of a wide variety, but today she wanted country and old rock.

Noon rolled around and her stomach reminded her she hadn't eaten.

The doorbell rang, earning a frown from her as she passed the hallway mirror, headed for the door. *Who could that be?*

She opened the door to find a young man smiling sheepishly on her doorstep holding a beautiful bouquet of mixed flowers. "Miss Matthews? Peyton Matthews?"

"Yes."

"These are for you. Sign here, please." He handed her a clipboard for her signature.

"Where did these come from?" she asked as she held it back out for him to take.

After he handed her the vase, he said, "There's a card attached."

The flowers were gorgeous. A huge mixed bouquet with daisies, roses, lilies and flowers she didn't even recognize, spread out in a great arrangement big enough to fill her doorway. "Wow. These are gorgeous. I wonder who they are from." Her hands shook, rattling the flowers in the vase as she moved to set them on the table. She hoped Charles hadn't found her. After she'd run from him a few years ago, she'd done her best to cover her tracks, but there was only so much one woman could do to protect herself.

Peyton now carried a concealed weapon just for that purpose.

Wetness coated her palms as she rubbed them down the thighs of the sweatpants she'd thrown on when she went to clean. Perspiration popped out on her forehead. She didn't want to open the card.

She inhaled sharply. *This is ridiculous. There's no reason to be scared. You've done your best to hide yourself. He would have a hard time finding you in Bandera, Texas.*

Capturing her bottom lip between her teeth, she bit down sharply to bring herself back into focus. The pain helped. She snatched the card from its plastic holder, folded the edge back and yanked it out.

The words blurred a little as she read the sweet card from the man she didn't want to have feelings about, but realized he was getting under her skin a little too quickly.

> *Thanks for last night. You're a sexy, gorgeous woman and I can't wait to love on you again.*
> *Love Jason*

"How sweet." The swooping in her belly calmed as she read the note again. Jason. She tapped the card against her lips. First the phone call. Then the flowers. What more should she expect from the man?

A smile played on her lips for the rest of the day as she finished cleaning her house, washing her laundry and getting ready for work. She needed to get some food. Her shift started soon. She had to be on top of her game tonight. Saturday's were pretty rowdy at the bar most weekends. Lots of cowboys and cowgirls got a little out of control. Even though it wasn't part of her job to bounce, being a woman, she still needed to know when to call in the troops should someone get too boisterous.

She put on her leather halter top and jeans before she slipped on her cowboy boots. Playing the part of cowgirl wasn't an easy thing for her, but it went with the persona the bar had so she'd do what she needed to. Her breasts were displayed enticingly above the cleavage of her top. The jeans showed off the soft curve of her hips and with the legs tucked into her pink and brown cowboy boots, she figured she played the part well enough.

The clock on the wall chimed eight-thirty, rousing her enough to realize she needed to get moving. The bar waited.

Music blared loudly as she waltzed through the door several minutes later, to find the place in full swing. Cowboy hats and rhinestone jeans took up most of the scenery. Neon lights in every kind of beer graced the wood walls. A band played in one back corner as the dancers two-stepped around the floor. Several people congregated in small groups laughing and having a good time. The place was packed even for a Saturday night.

"There you are. Good thing you're here. It's getting crazy," Dan said, wiping the bar on his end, keeping a close eye on the patrons of his establishment. He owned the bar along with his wife. The big, burly guy was like a father to her and too many of the other women who frequented the place. He seemed to take his job seriously. He didn't like it when some drunk cowboy started coming onto a woman who didn't want the attention.

"I'm on it, Dan." She swung around the bar's long expanse and immediately started working her way down the patrons sitting on her end to see what they needed. Faces blurred as she worked even though her thoughts were never far from the dark-haired cowboy she'd left standing on her porch early this morning.

Time sped by without her even being aware of how fast the clock was ticking until she wiped the sweat from the back of her neck.

"Hey babe."

She glanced up into the green eyes of a man she didn't know. "What can I get you?"

"You."

"Not for sale." She braced her hands on the bar. "What'cha drinkin'?"

"Whiskey straight up."

"Do you want one or two shots?"

"A shot at you."

"Lay off, buddy or I'll cut you off and have you bounced right out of here."

The man rapped his knuckles on the bar. "Fine, give me a shot then."

She poured his drink as she noticed an empty table across the bar the waitress hadn't cleared yet. Figuring she'd clear the glasses so they had more clean ones behind the bar, she wiped her hands and went around the bar's end to head for the table.

The minute she walked near the whiskey guy, he grabbed her around the waist and pulled her into his lap. "I told ya I wanted a shot."

"Let go."

"The lady said let go, mister."

She glanced up into the clear blue gaze of Jason. "I can handle him."

Jason ignored her. "I suggest you let go."

"Or you'll what, cowboy? Me and the lady were gettin' acquainted."

"Jason, I said I can handle this."

"You know him, little lady?"

"Yes, but that's not important. If you don't let me go in five seconds, you're going to lose a couple of teeth."

"I like my women feisty."

The man spun her around in his arms and tried to kiss her. She jammed her hand under his chin, gnashing his teeth together in a grind just as Jason landed a punch to the side. The man let her go as he grabbed his mouth and side simultaneously.

"Fuck!"

She backed up as the man rushed Jason, taking them both to the floor. Fortunately for Jason, the man apparently was already half drunk so he stumbled as they went down with Jason ending up on top. Jason swung, punching the man in the jaw. The man threw a punch, hitting Jason in the eye.

"Stop it!" She pulled on Jason's arm, trying to stop the brawl. "Stop." When they two men continued to throw punches at each other, she hollered for Dan and the bouncer.

The two men pulled Jason and the man apart, allowing them to rise from the floor. "Out. Both of you," Dan told them. "I don't want this kind of shit in my bar."

"But I was helping Peyton," Jason said, wiping the blood from his mouth.

"I can take care of myself, you dumbass."

"You didn't seem to be able to handle him very well, darlin'."

"Don't darlin' me. I had it under control whether you want to believe it or not."

"You needed me. Admit it."

"I didn't need you. I don't need you. Leave me the fuck alone!"

Hurt clouded his eyes, but she didn't care. He needed to know she could take care of herself. She'd made sure of that after the shit went down with Charles. He touched his quickly swelling eye with his fingertips.

"Fine. Call me whenever you get over yourself and realize you want to see me again." He wiped his mouth with the back of his hand before he turned to weave his way through the crowd to the door.

"Fight's over folks. Have a drink, dance, have a good time, but no more fighting," Dan said, pushing her back toward the bar. "You okay?"

"I'm fine."

"What's up between you and Jason Young?"

"Not a thing, why?"

"He seemed awful protective of you for some reason. Not that he wouldn't be around any woman getting manhandled, but I think there's more than meets the eye between you two."

"It's nothing, Dan. He's was being protective. Nothing more."

"Okay, honey, but if you want to talk, let me know. I have a good ear especially where those Young boys come into play. Ask Paige."

"Yeah, see where that got her? She's pregnant by one of them with twins."

He grinned and clamped a hand on her shoulder. "Yeah, but she's happy as a little pig in shit."

Rolling her eyes, Peyton grinned back. She'd give him that. Paige was definitely happy with her Young hunk.

After she took her spot behind the bar, she let her thoughts wander to the triplet who'd taken up residence in her mind for the last several months. *Damn him.* She glanced across the bar only to notice a couple of the other Young boys playing pool. Joshua stood off to one side of the table with the cue in his hands. She couldn't help but notice him since he looked just like Jason. Although she could tell the subtle difference between the two enough to tell them apart even from a distance. Jason carried himself a little differently. More confident? She wasn't sure, but there were definitely differences.

"Hey, can I get a beer?"

She dragged her thoughts back to the job at hand. She still had several hours to go before she could go home and lose herself in her fantasies again.

* * * *

Jason banged his hand on the steering wheel as he drove back toward the ranch. "Son of a bitch!" His hand throbbed from the beating it had taken just a short bit ago. His eye was almost swollen shut after the guy got a good punch off, hitting him in the left eye. He touched the swelling tissue and winced. "Fucker."

A bag of peas from the kitchen freezer would do for the swelling although it wouldn't help his damaged pride.

"What the hell is up with her anyway? I was trying to protect her and she went off on me like I was the one who tried manhandling her."

He didn't get women at all. Here he wanted to be her savior and she chewed him out for it. Didn't women want to be taken care of? Wasn't that what they were all about?

"I might need to talk to Mom on this one. I'm sure she could give me some advice on how to handle Peyton."

He drove through the main gates of the ranch, then up to the house. The light in the office glowed in the darkness so he knew his mother still sat at her desk even though the clock on the dashboard said ten. She really needed to knock off a little earlier, but tonight he needed to ask her advice on the matter of Peyton Matthews.

As he walked up the main lodge door, it opened and closed on its own, earning a frown from him. A chill went through him for a second as he kept walking toward the house. The ghosts around the place kept things lively even though they freaked him out a little sometimes. The cowboy who tended to hang around the main lodge seemed to be the most apparent, but there were others. A faint, distant childish giggle caught his attention for a second before he shook it off and kept moving. He had more important things to do than deal with ghosts tonight.

When he reached the office door, he knocked softly until his mother spun around in her chair. "Oh my. What the heck happened to you, Jason?"

"I got in a fight at the bar trying to protect Peyton."

His mother got up to head for the kitchen with him trailing behind like a lost little boy. "Let's get something to put on that eye before you lose sight in it completely." They moved through the double doors into the kitchen where the long cutting tables sat waiting for the morning meal. Two big walk-in refrigerator/freezers stood off to the left. His mother moved inside one and grabbed a plastic bag of peas. Once she had them wrapped in a cloth, she put it on his eye before she leaned back against the counter waiting for him to talk. "So what happened?"

"Well, I went to the bar after everything was done on the ranch today. I wanted to talk to her."

"You seem pretty friendly with her the other night."

"It's not a big deal, Mom."

"Are you sure?"

"Yeah. We're just having a good time."

"Okay, but I've heard that one before from Joel, Jeff, and most recently Jacob."

"I'm not falling into the trap of a relationship. That's not what this is about. She doesn't want anything and neither do I." He moved the cold sack away from his eye.

She grinned as she crossed her arms over her chest. "If you say so, Jason."

"It's the truth."

"All right, son. I believe you." She pushed his hand back so the frozen peas were on his eye again. "You were watching her while you were at the bar?"

"Well yeah, but just in between pool games with the other guys. Not like I was doing nothing more than watching her as she slung drinks." He shook his hand as his mother glanced at the raw knuckles. "She's really good, you know?"

"I imagine so. She does it for a living, right?"

"Yeah. She works there full time."

"So what happened?"

"Some guy hit on her when she came around the bar. I stepped in because he was all over her. The guy rushed me and we went down on the floor. He got in a couple of good punches before Dan broke it up."

"What did Peyton say about all this?"

"She got pissed off at me! I was trying to help her."

"I get the feeling she's a very independent woman, Jason. She probably thought she could handle the guy."

"That's what she said!" He threw up his hands. "I'll never understand women."

His mother laughed. "Maybe you should be having this conversation with your father."

"But how am I supposed to know how to handle her, Mom?"

"Don't handle her, Jason. She doesn't want you to."

"I don't understand."

"She wants someone to have a good time with. Nothing serious. Am I right?"

"Yeah, that's what she said."

"Then be the guy she wants. Don't force it. If you two are meant to be, then you will be."

"I don't want a permanent relationship, Mom. I'm not ready to settle down."

"Then don't worry about what you and Peyton have. If a good time is all you want, then that's what you should have, but I think there is a little more there than either of you want to admit. It'll happen in time."

He sighed as he put the bag on his eye. "This stuff is so complicated."

"Honey, if it wasn't, everyone would be doing it all the time."

"It was so much easier when I just took my pleasure from the whole thing and moved on. This stuff about giving a shit is for the birds."

"So you do care?"

"Maybe a little. I mean she's a nice girl. She's got her insecurities like any other woman, but I like to see her smile." He shook his head and glanced out the window. "Did you know she has a lot of piercings?"

"Like what?"

"A tongue ring, her ears, and her belly button. She also has a tattoo on her breast for her mother who died of breast cancer."

"Oh?" Nina smiled.

Shit. "I mean I saw it when she had her halter top on tonight at the bar."

She laughed. "Honey, I know you two were together the other night. You couldn't get away from the bonfire fast enough. I think I heard the bedsprings from your house clear over here."

"Sorry."

"Nothing to be sorry for. I'm glad you've found someone you connect with."

"Don't be planning a weddin'." A sneaky little grin spread across her mouth. "And no matchmaker stuff. I've seen your work with my brothers."

"I didn't do anything."

"No, just told Joel to stay away from Mesa, which he turned around to do the opposite. Jeff did the same thing with Terri. I'm sure you had a hand in Paige and Jacob too."

She shook her head innocently. "I didn't have a thing to do with Jacob and Paige. They found their way together without my help."

"But you don't deny interfering in meddling in the other two's relationships."

"Not at all. Those kids were meant to be together. You have to admit, they are much happier now that they've found love."

"True, but I'm not lookin' for love."

"No one is ever looking, Jason. It just finds us when the time is right."

"Well it's not the right time."

She patted his cheek with her hand right before she leaned in and kissed him. "If you say so, son."

Chapter Seven

Peyton sighed as the last of the patrons left the bar at two a.m. It had been a long night and the fight Jason had been in, didn't help. She found herself worrying about it after he'd left. His eye had begun to swell even before he disappeared. The blood on his lips bothered her too. She wanted to hold him, care for him, and the thought drove her nuts. She should call him, but then again she shouldn't. She didn't need him or so she kept telling herself. He could be the hero for some other woman. Not her. She didn't want him to be her hero, right?

"Well, tonight was an interesting night," Dan said, stopping next to where she stood putting clean glasses away.

"It sure was. Same Saturday night we always have, except a few fights tonight."

"One especially."

"Leave it be, Dan."

"He was protecting you, Peyton. Nothing a good man wouldn't do."

"Well I don't need a man to protect me. I take care of myself."

"I know, honey, but guys like Jason need to be the hero sometimes."

"He can be someone else's hero."

"He wants to be yours."

She let out a disgusted sound from deep in her throat, the sound almost like a sigh. She didn't want him to be her hero, right? Well maybe just a little. It was kind of nice to have a guy jump to her defense for a change. Jason didn't need to know that though. He needed to leave her the hell alone to give her some space.

"Think about it, Peyton. He's a good guy."

"I know he is, Dan. I'm not looking for a permanent fixture in my life though. I've got too many things going on to have time for a man."

"You need to make time. Jason isn't the type of man to wait around forever, honey. If you want him, you'd better go after him."

Dan walked back to the other side of the bar to fiddle with the cash register while she contemplated what he said. She knew Jason was a ladies' man. She watched him pick up women every weekend while she worked the bar, not that she was paying attention, mind you, but she'd see the women flock to him. He had a reputation for being good in bed and she could attest to that fact easy enough since he'd rocked her world the night before without much effort at all. Did she want more? She didn't know. The life she'd set up for herself didn't have room for a man in it on a long term basis, but she could do short term fling with him without too much effort on her part, sure enough.

As her cell phone started jingling in her pocket, she wondered who would be calling her this time of night. After she set down the glass rack in her hand, she grabbed it from her pocket and glanced at the screen.

Jason.

"Hey," she said, answering on the third ring. "How is your eye?"

"Fine. Listen I wanted to apologize."

"For what?"

"Trying to take care of your problem for you. I get you're the independent type and I overstepped my boundaries. I'm sorry."

"Did you have a talk with your mother?"

He laughed. "What makes you think so?"

"Because that sounds like something Nina would say. The few times I've had a chance to talk to her, she sounded like a very insightful woman."

"Okay, yeah, but it's true."

"All is forgiven."

"Are you sure? That was too easy."

"What can I say? I don't hold a grudge."

"Thanks." He cleared his throat. "How did work go after I left?"

She continued wiping glasses to put them away as she cradled the phone between her cheek and shoulder. "Smooth as every other Saturday night with a bunch of rowdy cowboys."

"That good, eh?" he asked, laughter in his voice.

"Yep, but at least I didn't get hit on again." She ran the dry towel over the surface of the bar.

"Too bad."

"Why do you say that?"

"I imagine you get hit on a lot."

"Actually, no, I don't. I think a lot of men are put off by my piercings and tats."

"I think they are sexy, especially your tongue ring when you sucked my cock."

"Bad boy."

"You like bad boys, don't you, Peyton?" he asked, his tone now gone serious.

"Yeah, kind of." Shivers rolled down her back as he dropped his voice into a low growl.

"Do you want me to come by your place tonight?"

"I think it's a bit late for any extracurricular activities tonight, don't you think, Jason? It is two in the morning."

"I'm up for it."

"I bet you are, cowboy, but I think I'll pass. I'm really tired since I didn't get to sleep in this morning and I cleaned house all day before I came to work."

"Sorry about the text earlier."

"No problem. It's fine. Oh, thank you for the flowers by the way. They're beautiful."

"It wasn't a big deal."

He almost sounded shy and unsure of himself on the phone. "It was to me. You'll never guess what?"

"What?"

"Those are the first flowers I've ever gotten."

"Really? A beautiful woman like you?"

"I guess I never found the right guy."

"I'm the right guy then."

"I suppose so." Silence stretched for several minutes while she continued to clean and stock before it was time to leave. "You still there?"

"Yeah."

"I better go. I'm almost done here and I need to head home."

"Let me walk you to your car."

She laughed as she blushed. "How? You're at home."

"No, I'm not."

"You're not?"

"I'm outside the bar."

"You've been out there this whole time we've been talking on the phone?" she asked, peeking out the blinds to see his truck sitting near the curb with him leaning on the hood talking on his cell phone.

"Yeah."

"You're a nut."

"Are you going to let me walk you to your car?"

"If you insist."

"I do."

"Let me grab my purse and I'll be right out."

"Okay. See you in a minute."

She clicked the phone shut as she shook her head. "The silly guy is standing outside by the curb talking to me on his cell."

"Sounds like he's smitten," Dan replied, heading toward the back office. "Bitten by the bug."

"I'm headed out."

"Okay. Be careful going home. I'll see you tomorrow."

"Yep. You be careful too. Talk to you then," she said, pushing open the door and locking it behind her with the key Dan had given her. She turned around to face the gorgeous man standing not ten feet from her. He made her breathless just looking at him. The floodlight on the street shadowed his face beneath his cowboy hat so she couldn't see his eyes, but she knew they stared right through her. She could feel the heat of his gaze without seeing his face. "Hi."

"Hi yourself."

"How's your eye?"

"Swollen shut almost."

"I'm sorry. You shouldn't have been hurt defending me."

"I wanted to or I wouldn't have."

"I can take care of myself."

"I know you can, babe, but I wanted to help and you shut me down."

"I don't need a hero."

"Yes you do and I want to be your hero."

"You don't understand. I haven't needed anyone for a long time."

"We all need someone sometimes."

"Not me."

"Yeah, even you." He ran his finger down her cheek. "Even a tough girl like you needs a man once in a while." His hand snaked around the back of her neck, pulling her in close. "I'm going to kiss you now."

"What about your lip?"

"My lip can handle a little lovin' from you."

"I'm glad because I want to kiss you too."

He tilted his head to the side as his lips brushed hers. She wanted more, so much more. The feel of his mouth brought with it the memories from his loving the night before. She found herself pushing her tongue into his mouth, capturing his tortured groan with her own. As they kissed, her world spun out of control. She'd come to need this man more than she ever thought possible in such a short time.

"Come home with me." She gasped as his hand found her breast.

"Are you sure?"

"Yes. I need you." He pushed his palm against the crotch of her jeans, grinding the stiff fabric into the engorged button between her legs. She moaned softly. "Please."

"Anything you want, darlin'."

"I want you."

"Let me walk you to your car and I'll follow you home."

"Okay." The breathless sound of her voice echoed in the dark night surrounding them. *God, I sound desperate, but I don't care.*

Within a few short minutes, they pulled into the driveway at her place as he parked his truck behind her. Was this crazy? She thought so, but really they probably only had tonight. He'd go on his way, find someone else to fuck on a regular basis, and she'd be alone...again.

The moment she stepped out of her car, he swept her up into his arms before he walked toward the front door. She squeaked as he picked her up, but ended up winding her arms around his neck. His scent drew her into his web of seduction as she found the crook of his neck with her nose. "You smell nice."

"Thanks. I showered before I came back to town."

"For me?" she asked when he stepped up on the porch.

"Yep. I needed to get the blood off my face and a shower felt good."

"I'm glad. Freshly washed cock is the best."

"You don't say?"

"Oh yeah." She fumbled with the key from her perch in his arms. He waited patiently as she jammed it into the lock and turned, then opened the door.

"We could always take another shower. I'm kind of partial to freshly washed pussy too."

Once he released her legs, she slid down his body, noting every bulge, muscle and contour of his impressive frame. "Oh, sounds like fun. I need one after the smoke and stink of the bar."

"Then let's share it. I'd like to soap every inch of you."

She took his hand, leading him toward the back where the bathroom stood off her bedroom. The place seemed small, but since it was just her, it didn't matter. Although, being such a big guy, the place felt even smaller. She'd bought the house with the inheritance from her mother when she passed. It was the only thing she owned outright, but it gave her the peace of mind knowing she always had a place to live.

"How long have you lived here?" he asked, following her to the bathroom.

"Not too long. A year or so."

"I thought you'd been in Bandera longer than that."

"A little. A couple of years is all though."

"Where'd you move from?"

"Can we not talk about me?"

"I want to know more about you."

"Why?" She turned on the shower and let the temperature adjust to warm as she stripped off her clothes.

He shrugged as he changed the subject. "I really like that top on you."

"I like it too."

Her clothing quickly found its way to the floor as she glanced at him through her lashes. "Are you going to shower with your clothes on?"

"Nope, but I'm enjoying watching you strip."

"You should have said so. I would have done a little strip tease for you."

"You did fine, darlin'."

Shivers raced down her back. She loved when he called her that. "Do I get to undress you?"

"If you'd like."

She bit her bottom lip as she concentrated on undoing each button down the front of his western shirt, one at a time, very slowly. His chest was such a sculpture of flesh, she wanted to trace every inch of it with her fingertips. With a sharp tug on the tails of his shirt, she released them from the waistband of his jeans.

What was it about Wranglers and a cowboy butt? She didn't know, but damn they sure looked good.

His belt came next as she tugged on the buckle to release it from the hole with a clank. "These things are pretty heavy."

"Yeah, but they do a good job of holding up a pair of jeans."

"I don't want it to hold anything up at the moment."

"Neither do I. I can't wait to feel you wrapped around me. It feels like it's been ages."

"It's only been a day."

He skimmed his hands down her arms as she worked on his belt. "I know, but I've been thinking about it all day. My dick has been so hard for you, I almost had to take care of my problem myself. I haven't had to do that for some time."

Once she had the zipper down, she shoved his pants to the floor, releasing the impressive length of his cock to her hand. She loved his cock. The length seemed to fit just right in her palm, her mouth or her pussy. A soft moan escaped his lips as she palmed him.

"Nice. I like when you make those soft little moaning sounds."

"Kind of like when you make the mewing sounds I like so much," he whispered, guiding her hand to the rhythm he liked as she cupped his balls. "Like a little kitten looking for its mother."

"This kitten has claws." She raked her nails down the length of his cock.

"Oh yes, she does."

He shivered, earning a smile from her. She loved torturing him beyond his control, just a little. It made him a man she could do such delicious things with and not feel guilty about her weird sense of need in the bedroom.

When she finally got him fully undressed, she turned toward the shower to step inside. Hot water cascaded down over her head as she dunked herself under the spray. Warm hands covered her breasts, kneading the flesh. He pinched her nipples between his thumb and first finger as she groaned deep in her throat. No mewing sounds when he did that. Those earned a hearty groan of satisfaction.

"Your breasts are very sensitive."

"Yes they are."

"I love them."

"I'm glad." She reached for his cock to palm the long, thick shaft, earning another moan from him. "I like your dick."

"Such a dirty mouth."

"No, I just believe in calling it what it is. It's a dick or cock and I enjoy it very much." A few pumps of her hand had him swelling even further while she managed to massage his balls.

"I love it when you touch my balls."

"Good." She dropped to her knees right before she enveloped his cock in her mouth. The indescribable sounds coming from his mouth made her hotter. She loved giving head to a guy who appreciated the talent a woman had when they sucked them off or just brought them to a higher plane of pleasure. She wouldn't suck him to completion this time. Nope. She wanted all his hard flesh deep inside her pussy when he exploded in rapture, but she'd make sure he was good and hard when that happened.

After several minutes, she stood again, taking his mouth with hers. She wondered if he thought it was sexy to taste himself on her tongue like she did. It made her hotter to taste her essence in his mouth when he went down on her. Too bad he wouldn't be able to do that in the shower. The confined quarters made it impossible.

Their tongues dueled from her mouth to his and back again in the most erotic dance she'd ever witnessed. She loved kissing him so passionately he lost control and ground his mouth against hers. Rough sex turned her on. Forcing a man to lose it while they had sex brought her desire to the peak.

When she finally moved her head to his ear, she growled. "Fuck me hard."

He grabbed her around the waist, lifting her until she could wrap her legs around his hips. His cock slipped into her pussy easily thanks to the cum dripping from her pussy. She wanted him so badly, she ached from it.

With her back braced against the tile wall of the shower, he fucked her so hard she groaned with each thrust of his hips.

"Play with your clit. I love to watch you come."

"It won't take much."

"Good. You come now, then we can fuck again in your bed after we finish the shower."

"I like it."

She reached down between them to finger her clit as he kept them fucking against the wall. The *slap, slap, slap* of wet flesh made her desire soar while she brought herself to brink with her fingertip massaging her clit. The friction was enough to send her over, but when he whispered, "Come for me," in her ear, she lost all control over holding back her orgasm.

She moaned his name in his ear as she spasmed around the thick cock inside her. Fullness stretched every inch of her pussy to accommodate the length and girth of his cock. He wasn't a small man by any means. It felt so good to have him inside her, she didn't want it to end, but end it would as he pumped his hips a few more times and filled her with his cum.

His whole body shook from the extent of his climax as he released her legs so she could stand on her own. "That was…"

"Awesome? Fantastic? Mind blowing?"

"All of the above, but I can't wait to do it again."

She grabbed the soap and began to lather up the hair on his chest. A little hair there just turned her inside out. These guys who waxed did nothing for her. "I love chest hair."

"Good thing I have some then, eh?"

She skimmed her fingernail over his nipples, watching in fascination as they pebble into hard points. Apparently, men had sensitive nipples too. "I like your chest. It's just right. Nice pecs. A little hair. Sensitive nipples. It's perfect."

"Thanks, but I really like yours."

The hair on his chest abraded her nipples deliciously when he leaned in and rubbed it across the tips of her breasts. "Oh. I like it when you do that."

"How about when I do this?" He dipped his hand between her thighs, pulling her pussy lips apart as he drove a finger into her.

Her breath caught in her throat. "Oh yeah."

"Let's take this into your bedroom," he said, slowly removing his finger from inside her.

She rinsed quickly and shut the water off. He grabbed two towels from the rack, handing her one to dry off with before he stepped out onto the bathmat. After he wrapped the towel around his tempting hips, he headed for the door as she quickly wiped the water from her body. She couldn't wait to get him between her thighs again. She had it bad it seemed, for one hunky Young brother.

Lordy, I'm in trouble.

Chapter Eight

Jason sat on his horse's back surveying the surrounding herd of cattle. Today was his turn to bring his family's herd down from the north pasture into the south area for grazing. It was a never ending thing with a cattle farm, but one he enjoyed immensely. He took a lot of pride in his work, but he hoped soon he would be able to leave working for his family and just do his own thing with his cattle and bucking bulls.

"Hey!" Jeff rode up beside him. "Is this all of them?"

"Yeah."

"Huh. Seems short. Did you count them?"

"Of course I counted them, dipshit. I'm not stupid."

"I didn't say you were, Jason. What bit you in the ass to make you so bitchy?"

"Nothing."

Jeff leaned on the pommel of his saddle with a grin across his lips. "A woman?"

Jason pushed his hat back on his head with his finger as he squinted into the afternoon sun. "Hell no."

"I know that voice. It *is* a woman. Let's see if I can guess who." Jeff leaned back and said, "Peyton Matthews?"

"Leave Peyton out of this." Jeff grinned, the silly fool. Just because he was happily encased in a relationship with a nice girl didn't mean the rest of them had to be.

"So it is her." He slapped Jason on the back, earning himself a punch in the arm. "Easy man. There's nothing wrong with being a little woman crazy."

"Speak for yourself."

"Got an itch to be between her pretty thighs, I'm guessing."

"Shut up, Jeff."

"What's wrong with that? We all need a little pussy once in a while, even you."

"I'm warning you. Back off."

"I bet it's been what? About a week since you've been inside her. I know the feeling, buddy. I need it at least a couple of times a week from Terri, otherwise I go batshit crazy."

"I don't need to hear about your sex life, Jeff. Let it be."

"But you're my brother. I'm giving you brotherly advice. Take the afternoon off and go get laid."

"You are letting me blow off work for pussy?"

"If you are as uptight as you sound, yeah. You need it." Jeff pulled his horse around to head back to the house. "Take my advice. Invite her over for dinner, a little wine, some flowers, you know. I'm sure I don't have to tell you how to wine and dine your woman."

"She's not my woman."

"But you want her to be or you wouldn't be all tied up in knots over her."

"No I don't. I don't need a woman."

"Yeah. Okay. Why don't I believe you, brother?" Jeff laughed as he kicked his horse into a gallop and headed back to the house.

"Fucker."

But what Jeff said had a ring of truth to it. He did want Peyton. Badly. It never seemed to get better either.

They no sooner made love and he wanted her again. *Whoa!* Where did that come from? Made love? He thought it was simply sex, but the more he thought about it, the more he realize yeah, it hard turned into making love with her, not just sex.

Wow.

He kicked his horse to circle the herd again to double check the count since it was his job to make sure they all made it down from the pasture.

A few minutes later, Joel rode up. *Jesus. What is this, get Jason a girlfriend day?*

"What's up, Joel?"

"Not much. I figured I'd check on you. You seem distracted at breakfast."

"I was. Got a lot on my mind."

"Oh yeah?"

"Yep." Jason leaned into the saddle, resting his forearm across the pommel.

"Like what?"

"Same shit, different day."

"Woman troubles?"

"Why the fuck does everyone think I'm having woman troubles? I'm not. I'm getting laid on a regular basis by a pretty gorgeous woman. We aren't serious so get that thought out of your head. It's just making love!"

One dark eyebrow rose over Joel's left eye. "Making love?"

"Having sex. Same thing."

Joel laughed as he tipped his cowboy hat forward on his head. "No it's not, brother. If you are calling it making love, you're in deeper than you think. Trust me on that one. I thought the same damned thing until

Mesa went home and I realized I didn't want to live without her."

"That's you, brother, not me. I don't need a woman and the woman doesn't need me. She's already told me as much."

"Did she?"

"Yeah. The night I got this nice shiner I'm still sporting the remnants of, when I tried to step in and help her at the bar. I don't need a hero, she said."

"Maybe she thinks she doesn't, but she really liked having you there for her."

"Don't get philosophical on me, Joel. It's not like you have a ton of women experience."

"I didn't need any when I found Mesa. I just knew."

"Oh yeah, like a bolt of lightning. You just knew she was the one."

"Well no, but talking to Mom helped. She showed me what I was missing if I walked away from Mesa."

"Mom has already given me the daughter-in-law speech."

"She has? Well then you are one step ahead of where you need to be. Peyton is a nice girl. You could do worse."

"But Peyton doesn't want anything beyond friends with benefits."

"Yeah, I thought that too, before Mesa walked away and I realized I didn't like the thought of her sleeping with anyone else."

Jason frowned as he took off his hat and swiped his fingers through his sweaty hair. It was hot today, even early summer in Bandera tended to be that way. "So what are you doing out here besides lecturing me on women?"

"Jeff asked me to relieve you so you could skip out and get laid."

"He's such a pain in the ass now that he's getting some regular like."

Joel grinned. "He has your best interest at heart and you know if you stay out here, Peyton is gonna find someone else soon enough to fulfill those desires swimming in her veins. She's a feisty one."

"Fuck that! She ain't getting some from anyone but me!"

The ring of Joel's laughter echoed off the rocks as Jason kicked his horse into a full gallop headed back to the main house. He quickly calculated in his brain how long it would take to unsaddle his horse, brush him down, head back to his house, get a shower in, and call Peyton with an invitation for dinner. He had approximately one hour to get everything done before it got too late to invite her.

He hoped she wasn't working the bar tonight. That would throw a whole new wrench in the plans.

When Jason rode into the barn, Jeff stood next to his horse, brushing the gelding down as he glanced over at Jason.

"Don't say a word."

"I wasn't going to."

"No, but I can tell you're thinking about it."

Jeff grinned, continuing to brush his horse down as he whistled softly under his breath.

The minute Jason had his horse's tack off, he quickly brushed the animal down and stabled him. Lucky for him, he hadn't worked the animal very hard today, and damn it, he was in a hurry.

Once he reached his truck, he slid inside, pulled out his cell phone and dialed Peyton's number.

"Hello?"

"Hey, babe."

"Hi Jason. What's up?"

"I thought we could get together tonight for a little dinner at my place."

"Dinner?"

"Yeah. I'll cook. I want to wine and dine you."

"Like a date?"

"Uh, sure. Why not?"

"Well, we really haven't been on a date."

"I know. I thought this was a good place to start."

She sounded unsure when she replied, "Uh, okay, I guess."

His heart plummeted into his belly, forming a knot he didn't like. "If you don't want to, just say so."

"No, I do, it's just…"

"What?"

"I had plans tonight."

"Plans?"

"Yeah."

She had plans. *What the fuck?*

"Like what? To wash your hair?" he growled. Surely she wasn't seeing anyone else, was she?

"I planned to spend the evening with a couple friends watching movies in our PJs, eating popcorn and ice cream, and just having a girl's night, but it's fine. I can cancel."

Relief washed through him. She wasn't seeing anyone else. "No, it's okay. We can do it some other night. I just kind of missed you this past week."

"You did?"

"Yeah."

He almost heard the smile in her voice. "I missed you too."

"Good. I'm glad I'm not alone in this mutual missing thing."

"So you want to date me, huh?"

"Well, yeah. I thought that's what we were doing anyway?"

"No, we've been fucking, Jason. There's a difference between dating and fucking."

"How about we do both?"

"I kind of like that plan. I mean, I miss having you in my bed, but I'd like to get to know you as a person too."

"How about tomorrow night?"

"I have to work the bar. I'm off on Tuesday though."

"Tuesday it is then. Plan on wearin' something sexy."

"Like?"

"A short skirt. A frilly top and no underwear."

"Oh, kinky. I like it."

"Can we meet for lunch or something before Tuesday? It's only Thursday."

"You'll survive without me until Tuesday, cowboy."

A low growl rumbled in his chest. "I don't want to. I'm pretty damned horny right now."

"So am I, but you'll have to have fun without me until then."

"Bullshit on that noise. I'll wait for you. Don't keep me waiting very long. I'm not a patient man when it comes to pussy."

"Damn, I wish I hadn't made plans tonight."

"Me either, babe, me either."

"I guess I'll talk to you later then," she whispered into the phone. "You know I'd kiss you silly right now if I was there. Slide my tongue along your neck, bite you on the shoulder. Fuck, I'm horny."

"Quit teasing me or I'll crash your party no matter who is there."

"Sheila."

"Sheila?"

"Yeah. That's who is coming over for our girl's night. Oh and Mandy. I also invited Paige even though she can't drink. We haven't had a chance to catch up lately."

"What are you going to watch?"

"Probably some chick flick with blubbering, hot men and nakedness."

"Oh?"

"Magic Mike or something."

"Isn't that like a stripper movie?" he asked, gripping the steering wheel. Why all of the sudden did he not like her looking at other men, sleeping with other men or anything else with another man. This was stupid. He didn't need to get involved with her on any regular basis.

Too late.

"I better go. The girl's will be here soon and I have to go to the liquor store for alcohol yet."

"Be good."

"I will. No worries there, cowboy. I kind of like the idea of a steady guy and a steady lay."

"You do? I thought you didn't want a relationship?"

"Who said anything about a relationship? Dating isn't a relationship."

"I'm the only man in your bed though."

"Yes, you are. I don't spread myself thin like that. There is no use sleeping with more than one. It gets kind of messy doing that. You know, keeping names straight and all."

"Peyton," he growled.

She laughed. "Bye, Jason."

The phone clicked in his ear. She had him tied up in knots and she was laughing about it like a schoolgirl. He wasn't sure he liked the way this thing was turning, but he wasn't sure how to stop it spiraling out of control.

* * * *

Peyton hung up the phone and smiled. Why the whole situation seemed to lift her spirits beyond the stars, she wasn't sure. She kind of liked having Jason Young wrapped around her little finger. He wanted her. That much was clear, but how much? A lot apparently.

Her phone rang again. This time Mandy's name came up on the caller ID.

"Are we still on?"

"Yep. There will be four of us."

"Four?"

"I invited Paige to hang out too although she can't drink."

"Okay. Are you going to get booze?"

"Yep. On my way there now."

"Who were you talking to before? Your phone went right to voicemail when I called a few minutes ago."

"Jason."

"Jason Young?"

"Yeah."

"Since when are you dating him? He's like a total playboy."

"Just recently. We've only done a few things together. Nothin' serious."

"A few things like what?"

"The shower. His bed. My bed."

"You fucked him?"

"Hell yeah. Fabulous sex with a hot guy. Are you kidding me?"

"Wow."

She chewed her bottom lip for a minute wondering whether she should ask what was on her mind. *What the hell.* "You haven't done him, have you, Mandy?"

"Hell no. Not that I wouldn't given the chance, but I've never had the occasion to."

Peyton exhaled sharply and answered, "Good."

"You were totally worried, weren't you?"

"Uh, yeah. He's been with a lot of women in this town. I'm just not sure who."

"I don't know if he's done Shelia though. You'll have to ask her."

"I'm not sure if I want to know. I mean, that was before me, right?"

"Sure it was, honey. Sure it was."

She didn't like where her thoughts were headed. "I'm going to go so I can hit the liquor store. See you in about two hours."

"Sure. I'm bringing the popcorn. Sheila has the ice cream. What is Paige bringing?"

"Chips and dip."

"Awesome. Lots of junk food to eat while we watch some chick flicks."

"Talk to you in a bit."

"Sure. Bye."

She hung up the phone and then pressed it to her forehead. Her thoughts went haywire thinking about

Jason with another woman even though she knew he'd been with plenty. It didn't mean she had to like it. Nope, not one bit.

When she pulled back into her driveway about an hour later, she noticed Paige sitting on the porch with a bottle of water. "Did I tell you the wrong time?"

"No, I figured I'd come early."

"What's wrong? You look like you've been crying."

"Nothing. I got into a fight with Jacob. That's all."

"Hang on. Let me open the door. We'll get something to drink and you can tell me about it." Peyton opened the front door, bringing the bags of alcohol with her. She'd offer Paige a drink, but she knew that wasn't going to work with her being pregnant and all.

"So what happened?" she asked as she set the bottles on the counter in the kitchen.

She liked her small house on the edge of town. She couldn't have animals or anything there without fencing off part of the yard, but she had a little porch with a couple of rocking chairs on it, a nice living room with leather furniture, a modern kitchen with granite countertops and stainless steel appliances, two bedrooms and two bathrooms. The yard wasn't very big, but she had a garden with some flowers so she was happy.

Paige was quiet for several minutes, but she didn't want to push. Peyton arranged the bottles on the counter to give herself something to do. Being the woman friend felt foreign to her so she wasn't sure how to handle this situation, but when she heard a muffled sob coming from her friend, she turned around to take her in her arms. "It'll be okay."

"I'm not so sure."

"What did you fight over?"

Tears rolled down Paige's face, making Peyton choke up herself, before she blurted out, "He wants two boys!"

Peyton did a double take. "You fought over the sex of the babies?"

"Yes. He insists that it's two boys. I think it's two girls even though I want one of each. We got in a huge fight and he walked out. He left, Peyton. What if he doesn't come back?"

"Honey, listen to yourself. This is silly. He loves you. Besides, what difference does it make whether the babies are boys or girls? You'll love them no matter what sex they are and so will he."

"I'm being silly, huh." Paige sniffed as she wiped the tears on her face.

"Yes you are, but it's hormones, honey. You're full of them right now and everything that man says is either going to piss you off or make you love him all the more."

"You're right. This is silly. I'm going to call him." Paige grabbed her purse and then wiped her face as she pulled out her phone.

Peyton went into the pantry in the corner to get the cups and other things they would need as she listened to the one-sided conversation from Paige to Jacob. "Hi, honey. I'm so sorry I got so upset with you. It's my fault. Peyton says it's the hormones, but I wanted you to know I don't care whether the babies are boys or girls. I love you. I want a family with you."

Apparently Jacob made her cry again as Paige began to sniff back tears.

"I love you too. No, I'm okay. I won't be driving tonight. I'm staying at Peyton's. Okay. I'll see you in the morning."

She heard Paige hang up as she arranged the chips in a bowl and mixed the onion dip into the sour cream. "All better?"

"Yeah. Sorry."

"No problem. That's what friends are for."

"So what is going on between you and Jason?"

"Nothing. Why?"

"I heard you two had raunchy sex at his place last week."

"Where did you hear that?"

"Jacob."

She jammed her hands on her hips. *Men!* "Man, those boys don't know how to keep anything a secret, do they?"

"They're brothers. They talk amongst themselves especially when it has to do with a woman."

"What else did Jacob say?"

"That you two looked cute together." Paige popped a chip into her mouth. "Are you dating?" she asked, in between bites.

"I wouldn't call it that yet."

"So just non-committal sex?" Paige asked, taking another chip and dragging it through the French onion dip.

"Yep," she said as she shooed Paige away so she could set the bowls on the table.

"How is he?"

"Um, fine. Why?"

"I mean is he good in bed?"

"I would say so although I don't have a lot to compare to." She blushed to the roots of her hair at the admission. Why she felt she couldn't just say it without blushing, she wasn't sure. It wasn't something to be ashamed of, right? "Good God! I don't ask you how Jacob is in bed. What's with the questions?"

"I just wondered since he has such a reputation with the women in Bandera."

"Yeah, I know." She slapped the spoon on the table. "I don't need to hear about it."

Paige raised her hands. "Easy girl. I was just askin'."

"Well don't ask. I don't care who he's slept with. He's with me at the moment and that's all that matters."

Paige wrapped her arms around Peyton's shoulders and pulled her in for a hug. "Yes it is."

The doorbell rang and Peyton went to answer it, expecting Sheila and Mandy any minute. The other two ladies were standing together at the door when she opened it up. "Come in."

"Where's the booze?" Sheila asked, making a beeline for the wine bottle on the counter. "I need a drink."

"What's up with her?" Peyton asked Mandy as she shut the door behind them. "It's not like her to jump into the alcohol so fast."

"She's had a rough day. She just found out about you and Jason."

Chapter Nine

Peyton knocked on the bathroom door after Sheila took one of the bottles of wine and locked herself in. "Sheila?"

"Leave me alone, Peyton. I hate you."

"Then why the fuck did you come to my house?"

"Because you're one of my best friends." The sound of a sob broke through the pane of the door.

"I don't get you at all."

"I love Jason Young and you're fucking him."

"Oh please. You do not love him. You went out with him what? Once or twice?" Peyton tapped on the door again. "Come out of there."

"Not until I'm good and drunk so I don't punch you."

Peyton leaned against the wall near the door, sipping a glass of wine she'd poured before she went after Sheila. *This whole thing is stupid.* "Try it, babe. We can go round all night if you want. I'm game. I haven't been in a fight lately."

"You'd hit me?"

"If you hit me first, yes."

"What a bitch."

"You're in my house, drinking my wine, and you're calling me a bitch?"

Silence.

The lock clicked right before the door slowly opened. "I'm being stupid, aren't I?"

"Yes, you are. Besides, there's nothing between me and Jason other than some hot sex." Peyton wasn't sure she wanted to know, but she asked anyway. "Did you fuck him?"

Sheila bit her lip.

"You did." The jealousy Peyton felt surprised her. Surely she wasn't upset that Jason had slept with Sheila, was she? Maybe. But why? They were only having a good time, right?

"Yeah. Twice."

"I'm not sure I want to know."

"Why not? You asked." Sheila walked past her into the living room and then spun around. "You aren't jealous, are you?"

Peyton folded her arms over her chest. The protective stance didn't fool her friends though as Sheila, Mandy and Paige looked on. "No."

"Yes you are! You totally are!" Sheila flopped down on the couch as she brought the wine bottle to her lips. After she swallowed, she said, "You're in love with him."

"No, I'm not. We're fucking. That's it."

"I can see it in your face."

Peyton glanced at Paige who shrugged and Mandy who nodded. "You all are full of shit. I'm not in love with him. We are just two people finding solace in each other's company. That's it."

"Then don't fuck him anymore," Sheila said, taking another swig from the bottle.

"But I don't want to stop making love with him. We're good together. He's the best I've had in a long time."

"Do you hear yourself?" Mandy asked, taking a seat next to Sheila on the couch, reaching for the wine bottle.

"What?"

"You said making love, not having sex, not fucking, making love." She pointed at Peyton with the bottle top before she took a long drink. "You are totally in love with him."

"We aren't discussing this anymore. I'm done. I'm not in love with him. We are fucking, that's it. Nothing more." She glanced at Paige who stood nearby with a little smile playing on her lips. "What?"

"You sound like me before I realized I had it bad for Jacob. Now look at us, expecting twins."

"You totally fell the minute you saw him."

"The minute I saw him, he was drunk off his ass and getting it kicked by three other guys. Then he came back after puking in the hall at the bar, with throw up on his shirt. Not a good first impression, Peyton."

"True, but once you hauled him across the street, paid for his room so he could sober up, you were hooked."

"Yeah, no and stop trying to change the subject of you and Jason. I can attest the Young brothers are definitely worth the trouble, but make sure you don't get hurt. Jason is a player. He always has been."

"I know, Paige. I've watched him enough at the bar to know his game."

"Then make sure you don't fall into it. If he's playing you, then blow him off. Don't get me wrong, I love all of Jacob's brothers, but there are several of them that are into seeing how many women they can fuck in a year." She glanced at Sheila from across the room. "No offense, Sheila, but he used you if you fucked him."

Sheila took another swig from the bottle. "I know."

"Enough of this talk. We were supposed to be having a good time, not talking about who we are fucking this week." Peyton grabbed the bottle of wine, then poured herself more into the glass she held. "What are we eating, ladies? We can call for pizza or go for burgers, although not a good idea since we've been drinking."

"I could drive. I can't drink anyway," Paige said, skimming her hand down her gently rounded stomach.

"You are so cute with your belly," Sheila replied, her words beginning to slur.

"Thanks. I'm glad I didn't have too much morning sickness with this pregnancy. I was afraid of that when I found out it was twins."

"How are you going to handle two babies at once without family help?"

"Nina has already promised to help me a lot with them. She's excited about having more grandbabies."

"Do you know what they are?" Peyton asked, sipping her wine. "I mean the sexes?"

"Not yet. We go for an ultrasound in a couple of weeks."

"What are you hoping for?"

"One of each. I think it would be great to have a boy and a girl. Nina wants girls." Paige laughed. "She already has the boys so she's hoping for at least one girl in the mix. Plus having nine boys, she really wants granddaughters."

"I really like Nina. She's a hoot," Peyton said. "I've had the chance to talk to her some while at the feed store and things. We've even had lunch a couple of times together."

"She's bringing you into the fold," Paige replied.

"What do you mean?" Peyton didn't like the thought of being manipulated.

"She's a sneaky one. I think in her roundabout way, she's setting up women she likes to get her boys married off." Paige shifted in the chair so she faced Peyton. "She was very sweet to me before Jacob and I got together. We kind of found our way together without much help, but as soon as she knew we were seeing each other, she totally jumped onboard with our relationship."

"Oh, she's definitely sneaky."

"She never helped me when I was dating Jason," Sheila whined.

The sound grated on Peyton's nerves. She really didn't want to compare her *relationship* such as it is, with Sheila's. It was bad enough Jason slept with her. This was something Peyton would have to deal with for however long they were together, but she didn't want to be constantly reminded of it. "Maybe she didn't think you were the right person for him?"

"And you are?"

"Hell if I know, Sheila." Peyton shrugged, sipping her wine. Sheila was three sheets to wind or getting close and she didn't really want to get into some kind of a brawl with her friend over a guy. "We are having a good time, nothing more. It's still very early for anything to be even called a relationship."

"How many times have you fucked?"

"Does it matter?"

"Yes it matters, to me."

"I'm not telling you an exact amount. We did it several times at his house."

Sheila jumped to her feet, spilling wine from the bottle on the carpet. "At his house? He took you to his house?"

Okay, this is getting out of control.

"Well, yeah. After I'd been to the muddin' party. He resisted a lot, for some reason I'm not quite sure of even now, but he finally gave in."

"You threw yourself at him? You are a fucking slut!"

"Okay. I'm tired of your mouth, Sheila. What is going on between me and Jason has no reflection on you or what you had. You slept with him. Unfortunately, it's something I have to deal with, but I'm not a slut. I haven't been with a shit ton of guys. Yes, Jason and I fucked. It was good. It was fabulous. The best I've ever had, but it doesn't mean I'm a slut. Take it back!"

"I will not! You went to the muddin' party with Aaron and ended up sleeping with Jason? That's what I call a slut."

"I'm calling you a cab."

"I'm not leaving until we've had this out."

"Girl, there is nothing to have out. Jason didn't want you past however many times you had sex. He still wants me after several times. Get over it!" Peyton set her glass down and stood to retrieve her cell phone. She needed to get Sheila out of her house before something happened to ruin their friendship altogether. With her cell phone in hand, she dialed the local cab company phone. She kept them on her cell phone for patrons at the bar. "Yeah, I need a cab at…" She rattled off her address and closed the phone. "They'll be here in fifteen minutes."

"I told you I'm not leaving." Sheila shoved Peyton, pushing her back a few steps.

"Don't do this, Sheila."

"He's mine."

"No, he's not. For the moment, he's mine." Sheila shoved her again, pushing her into the end table where her glass of wine sat, spilling the contents. "Enough, Sheila. You can get your bag and sit out on the front porch to sober up."

"This is total bullshit." Tears welled up in Sheila's eyes. "I love him."

"No you fucking don't. You went on like two dates. That's it."

"I can fall in love in such a short amount of time."

"I did," Paige answered. "I denied it, but I was totally in love with Jacob very quickly."

"You aren't helping matters here, Paige."

"Sorry."

"See! Paige loved Jacob that quickly. I can totally be in love with him."

"You are not, Sheila. Besides, he doesn't love you."

"You think he's in love with you?"

"There isn't love here. It's mutual sexual satisfaction, nothing more, at least for now. I don't love someone in a few days."

"But he took you home."

The whine coming from her friend made her ball her hand into a fist. She hated whiny people.

A honk sounded outside. "Take the cab and go home. You need to sleep this off."

"Fine, but I'll remember this conversation and we'll be having this out sooner or later, Peyton."

"Whatever, Sheila. It doesn't matter."

Sheila grabbed her purse before she opened the front door. "Yes, it does. He's mine."

Peyton shook her head and rolled her eyes as Sheila shut the door behind her. "Wow."

"Yeah, wow," Mandy said, taking another sip from the bottle Sheila left on the coffee table.

"How about you get a glass?"

"I'm redneckin' it tonight."

"Not in my house." Peyton grabbed a wine glass from the rack in the dining room and handed it to Mandy. "If you're going to drink here, you drink from a glass."

"Sheila wasn't."

"I'm not sure what her deal was, but I'm glad that's over with. It was getting crazy."

"You know you shouldn't have taken her man."

Peyton mopped up the wine from the table with the towel she'd retrieved from the kitchen. "Don't you fucking start or you can leave too."

"I'm just sayin…"

"Well knock it off! I didn't steal her man. Jason wasn't dating her when we started seeing each other, so I didn't take him away from her."

"So you are dating?"

"Fuck if I know what this is. We slept together a couple of times. He wanted to have me come over for dinner tonight at his place, but we already had plans for our girl's night."

"I'd call that a date," Paige said, chomping on some chips sitting on the coffee table.

"I suppose, but it hasn't happened yet."

"I've never heard of him dating anyone for more than a month or so," Mandy added, eating a couple of chips herself.

"It doesn't matter. I'm playing this out for whatever it's worth. I'm not looking for a husband and he's not looking for a wife so we're on the same page there."

"Good for you. I don't think he'd make good husband material from what I know of him," Mandy said. "But I don't know him that well either."

"I don't think any of the Young brothers were looking for wives when they hooked up with their respective mates. I know I wasn't looking for a husband and babies when we got together. It just happened."

Peyton poured herself more wine, emptying the first bottle of many she'd purchased for tonight. Maybe it was a night to get drunk. She might. It had been a while since she'd allowed herself to let loose and hang out with the girls. Of course, this night hadn't started very well with Sheila and her drama.

"If it happens, it happens. I'm not looking for it is all I'm saying."

"So what are we having for dinner?"

"Pizza sounds really good to me, right now," Paige replied. "With ranch dressing."

"Eeewwww!" The other two said in unison as they all laughed together.

An hour later found them watching Magic Mike on television with three pizza boxes between them. Paige had her cheese with ranch dressing, satisfying her pregnancy cravings, as Peyton and Mandy had their own concoction of whatever they wanted on their pizzas. No ranch dressing here. The movie had lost interest for Peyton after the first few minutes. Yes, Channing Tatum is hot, but Jason was homegrown cowboy built without the gym to supplement his muscles. Although, she had seen a weight set sitting in the corner of his bedroom so he apparently did some working out.

She wasn't sure why he held such fascination for her, but he did from the first moment she'd laid eyes on him at The Dusty Boot. The drawl of his words, the way he filled out his T-shirt or western shirt, the size of his arms, the trimness of his waist, the long legs in those boot-cut Wranglers, and oh, his butt was to die for.

"Peyton?"

"Sorry, yeah?"

"Mandy asked you a question. You seemed lost in thought. Aren't you enjoying the movie?" Paige asked, biting into the last piece of pizza on her plate.

"Oh, it's great."

"What was the last thing Channing Tatum said?"

"Uh…"

"You don't even know, do you?"

She blushed as she set her plate on the table. "No."

"It's bad when he can't even hold your attention." Mandy grabbed another slice. "What were you thinking about or should I ask who?"

"Jason."

"Well duh," Paige answered. "I could tell the by the look in your eyes. The faraway gaze gave it away. Nina says I get the same look when I'm thinking about Jacob too."

"Well you should. You're in love with him."

"Are you admitting you're in love with Jason?"

"No. In lust, yes."

Mandy scooted closer to the table, crossing her legs under her as she focused on Peyton. "What is he like?"

"You want me to give you details?"

"Hell yeah, baby. Spill it!"

Could she really give them details of making love, no, having sex with Jason? Maybe. What was it about women wanting to know what it's like between two people? "Details?"

"I'm living vicariously through the two of you. I haven't been with a guy in six months," Mandy shared.

"Six months?"

"Yep and even then, it wasn't great. He was pretty quick and not much into foreplay."

"That sucks," Peyton said.

"Exactly, now spill. I want to know what it's like with those Young boys. Maybe I'll hook up with one just to see."

"There are a couple who aren't tied down yet." Peyton laughed. "Maybe you could hook up with one of them."

"Maybe I just might. You never know." Mandy blushed. "I could do with finding me a good man who knows what the hell he's doing in the sack. I'm tired of this shit with these losers." She pushed against Peyton's shoulder. "So tell me."

"Well, he definitely knows how to eat a girl out."

"Seriously? I've mever had a guy do that to me before."

"You're missing out then. I love when a guy goes down on me. His mouth down there licking, sucking, and when he shoves those fingers inside you, holy shit!"

"Yeah?"

Peyton noticed Paige blushing from her seat across the room. "Right, Paige?"

"Yes," she whispered, covering her cheeks. "I can't talk about this stuff."

"And?" Mandy asked. "Do you come?"

"Oh yeah, several times if he's into doing it right."

"Shit, really? Hell, I'm lucky to come once with a guy."

Peyton sat back against the rear of her chair. "You've been dating the wrong guys, then. You need to find one who is into what makes you tick."

"Wow." Mandy's sigh of the word made Peyton smile.

It sure was wow with Jason.

"What about when he actually sticks his cock in there?"

"It's like being filled up to the brim." Peyton shifted on the chair as she remembered the feeling. She'd been horny before, but all this talk wasn't making it any better.

"What's the best position?"

"Against the wall."

"Holy shit! Against the wall?"

"Uh yeah. He gets so deep, it's like amazing."

"What about your G spot? Have you ever had him hit that?" Mandy shook her head. "I think it's hogwash myself. I'm not sure it even exists."

"Oh it does." Peyton knew it was there. Jason has it hit several times during their raunchy sexcapades, but when her back had been against the wall...oh yeah, he'd hit it big time.

"Yeah?"

"Definitely. Trust me, it's there. You just have to have the right angle of penetration."

"Okay, now I want to sleep with Jason," Mandy said with a laugh.

"Not happenin', girlfriend."

"I was kidding, Peyton, but maybe one of his brothers." She glanced at Paige. "Is Jacob good too?"

"He is with me." Paige blushed again. "I mean we are good together, yes, but I don't know if he'd been that way with anyone else. It helps we are in love." She pointed at Peyton. "Not that you can't have good sex without being in love. You know?"

"I don't think you have to be in love to have great sex, but it helps if the guy gives a shit about your pleasure. If he's all about himself, you aren't going to get much out of it. Believe me, I've been with some losers too."

"How do they compare with Jason?"

"They don't. Not even close."

"You know. I think he's totally in love with you," Paige said.

"Why do you say that?" Peyton asked, taken aback by Paige's revelation. Surely it wasn't true.

"Because I've never seen him in this good of a mood. The last couple of days he's been whistling while he works, smiling a lot more and everything."

"It doesn't mean he's in love with me. We've had a discussion, him and I, and neither of us is looking for anything other than a good time."

"Then why are you dating him?"

"To see."

"See what?"

Peyton wasn't sure how to answer Paige's question. What was she looking for in the relationship with Jason? Surely she wasn't looking for love, right?

Well maybe.

"I don't know, really."

"I think you're half in love with him already."

"I can't be, Paige. I've only been seeing him for like a week."

"But you've known him for several months. You've seen him at the bar, how he interacts with his parents and his brothers, how he takes care of others around him and the hot sex is just a bonus." Paige nodded. "Yep, you're in love with him, all right."

"I am not."

"Are you having trouble keeping your mind on things other than him?"

"Sometimes."

"You think about him all the time?"

"Sometimes."

"You can't wait to see him again?"

"Sometimes." Peyton shook her head. "I'm not in love with him."

Paige shrugged and sipped her soda. "If you say so."

They let the movie continue to run as Peyton thought about the conversation. Yeah, she thought about him *a lot*. Yeah, she wanted to be with him night and day. She wanted to find out more about him, his dislikes, his interests, what made him tick, but she wasn't in love with him, right? People didn't fall in love with someone in a week?

Chapter Ten

Tuesday rolled around and Jason was nervous. He wasn't sure how this evening would go with Peyton, but he had high hopes they would end up in his bed. It had been too long without, even though it had only been not quite a week without her hot little pussy around him.

He'd been to the bar each night she worked, just watching. He loved how she interacted with her customers, smiling most of the time. There had been a couple of times he wanted to step in when she had a particularly rowdy patron, but he didn't. He stayed in his spot in the booth near the back, just watching.

She was beautiful no matter what she wore, how she had her hair, how much makeup she had on or whatever. She twisted his guts into knots.

When the doorbell rang, he wiped his sweaty palms on the thighs of his jeans, checked everything was in its place on the table waiting for their intimate dinner to commence and headed for the door.

He knew he had a shit eating grin on his face that slowly slid off when he opened the door.

"Sheila?"

"Can I come in?"

"Uh, sure. I guess. I'm having company soon."

"I know. Peyton is coming over. I wanted to be here when she got here because this is something you should both hear."

"I don't like the sound of this."

"You probably won't when I tell you what's up."

"Why don't you just tell me what's the problem."

"No. Peyton needs to know."

The doorbell rang again as dread now slid through him. He didn't like the way Sheila was looking at him and he sure didn't like the glaze in her eyes. She almost looked like she was high or drunk.

He opened the door to find Peyton on the other side. "Hey." He kissed her quickly on the lips.

"Hey." She stepped inside the house and he shut the door behind her. "Sheila here? I saw her car outside."

"She just got here," he whispered. "I don't know what's up, but she insisted you be here when she told me why she's visiting."

"I can totally hear you."

"Why don't we all take a seat in the living room so you can share with us what your visit is about, Sheila."

"Fine." Sheila took a seat in the chair across from the couch.

He took one of Peyton's hands and led her to the couch so she could sit beside him. Somehow he thought this was going to affect both of them and he wasn't sure he liked the feeling. Right now, he wanted to shove Sheila out the door, lock it behind her and lose himself in Peyton's arms.

"What's this all about?"

"Peyton knows we slept together."

"So? I don't keep things from her, but I don't necessarily enjoy telling her about other women I've been with."

"And you told me you'd slept with him when you were at my house last week."

"That was before I found out something today that has changed everything."

"What?" Jason asked, his gut twisted in a knot.

"I'm pregnant."

"What?" He jumped to his feet. "That's impossible."

"We didn't use a condom, Jason."

He raked his fingers through his hair. This was nuts. She couldn't be pregnant. "You said you were on birth control."

"I wanted you. I would have said anything to get you into bed with me."

He glanced down at Peyton. Her face had turned ashen. "Peyton?"

"I think I'd better go. This is between you two."

With both of her hands in his, he pleaded, "No. Stay, please. I need you here."

"You need to talk and decide what you're going to do about this, Jason. It doesn't concern me."

"Yes, it does. You're part of my life now."

"We're only dating."

"Not to me. I need you here."

Sheila jumped to her feet with her hands on her hips. "This is all so touching, but what the hell are you going to do about me? I don't want to have a baby out of wedlock."

"I'm not marrying you, Sheila, if that's what this is all about."

"I don't want a bastard child."

"If the baby is mine, I'll take care of it, but I'm not marrying you. I don't love you."

"If? You think I was fucking around with more than just you?"

"Hell, I don't know what you've been doing. If you gave it to me so easily, you could have been with a half a dozen guys at the same time."

Sheila's hand snaked out and slapped him across the cheek. "How dare you. I'm not a slut unlike someone else in this room who slept with you after going to a party with another guy."

"Leave Peyton out of this."

"I won't. She's standing between the two of us."

"There is no you and me, Sheila. I won't be blackmailed into marrying you because you *might* be pregnant with my child. As I said, if it turns out to be mine, and yes, I will insist on a paternity test, then we'll deal with it, but I'm not marrying you."

"You haven't heard the last of me." Sheila stomped to the door, whipped it open and left in a huff.

"Are you okay?" Jason asked, taking Peyton in his arms. He wasn't sure how this would affect his budding relationship with the woman in his arms, but he didn't like how quiet she had become or the paleness of her complexion.

"I'm okay."

"I didn't see this coming."

"I know you didn't."

He moved to the front and shut the door. When he returned to her side, he sat them both down on the couch together. "I'm sorry. This is not something you should have to deal with. I need more information from Sheila like how far along she is. It's been a while since we've been together."

"Like how long?"

"A few months anyway." He glanced at the ceiling as he tried to remember. "Three months at least."

"She never mentioned anything to me when she was at my house drinking like a fish last week either and she knew you and I had been together."

"Somehow I think this is a ploy. If she is indeed pregnant, it's probably not mine. She'd have to be several months along for it to be."

"Do you think she's lying?"

"Could be. I mean, she sure jumped on me marrying her. Maybe she thought she'd get a ring from me and then play at a miscarriage. She wouldn't be the first to pull that kind of stunt."

"Why would she want to do that?" Peyton asked, sitting back against the arm of the couch.

"To break us up."

"I thought she was my friend."

"Some women do nasty things when men are involved."

A smile curved her lips as one eyebrow rose over her eye. "And men don't?"

"Maybe."

"I've seen some men do silly things too for a woman they were head over heels for."

"Oh, like what?"

"Cook them dinner."

"That's not a big deal. I'm cooking you dinner tonight," he whispered, sliding his lips along her neck. *Lord, I like to nip at her skin.*

Her breathing hitched. "Fuck them against the wall."

"Really?" he asked, liking where this conversation was headed. Fucking her against the wall sounded like a fantastic idea. He'd sure liked it when they'd done it before. He could hit the exact right spot inside her with that angle. "Wanna fuck?"

"More than anything."

He tugged her tank top over her head, revealing the lacy bra covering her breasts. *She sure has pretty tits.* "I like your boobs."

"Thanks."

He skimmed his mouth down her chest to capture a nipple in his mouth through her bra. "They are magnificent."

"I'm glad you like them."

"They are perfect for me. Just the right size for my hands to cup. Someday I want to fuck you between these gorgeous mounds."

"As I suck the head between my lips."

"Fuck yeah." He pushed one hand down the waistband of her jeans.

"Unbutton them first. It's easier to reach me." The minute he had them unfastened, she shoved them and her panties over her hips, revealing the tuft of hair at the juncture of her thighs. She toed off her boots as she wiggled out of her clothes. "Touch me. I need you."

Her hot pussy almost scalded his fingers as he pushed them inside her. His cock ached to be there. His balls burned for release. He wanted to fuck her on the kitchen counter.

Without breaking he sweat, he picked her up and headed for the kitchen. She squeaked when the cold countertop hit her butt cheeks.

He chuckled as he unbuckled his belt. "I'm going to fuck you hard and fast."

"Good. I'm so horny, I could combust."

"Open for me, babe. I'm comin' home."

He positioned his cock at her entrance and slowly slid the engorged flesh inside of her. The hot, silky feel of her pussy welcomed him like no one else ever had.

"That's it. Fuck me."

He slowly drew his cock out until just the head remained. She whimpered as she grabbed his hips, trying to pull him back inside her. With his hands on her hips, he began a slow, torturous fucking that would leave them both breathless, but wanting more. "Slow."

"No, fast. Hard."

"Nope. I'm controlling this."

The soft mewling sounds she made ramped his desire higher. She was perfect for him in every way. She met him stroke for stroke, touch for touch, and feeling for feeling, or at least he hoped so because he was losing the battle to keep his heart out of the mix with her.

* * * *

The hard slide of his cock pushed her closer and closer to the edge of insanity. She wanted him to fuck her harder, but then again, she didn't. The slow glide of his pace brought her to the brink without pushing her over. It was driving her crazy!

"Jason, please."

"Please what, darlin'?"

"Fuck!"

"Yeah, that's what we're doin'."

"You're killing me."

"I'm loving you."

"God, please. Fuck me harder. I need you so bad." With his finger nudging her clit, she exploded on a climactic high she'd never experienced before. "Oh God! Yes, yes, yes," she panted with each penetration. He grabbed her hips, slamming his pelvis against hers with each thrust, but he wasn't hitting quite the right spot for her to come again. She wanted that elusive G spot orgasm, but the angle wasn't right. "Wait!"

His movements came to a screeching halt. "What?"

"Something isn't right."

"Feels right to me."

"No, the angle. It's not right. You aren't hitting the right spot."

"What can I do?"

"Up against the wall. That worked last time, with my legs over your arms."

"Right, baby."

She wrapped her legs around his hips as he swung them both around. "Shower. Wall."

"Okay." He walked the few steps down the hall it took to get to the bathroom.

At least this way if she squirted all over, it wouldn't get on anything but the shower. She wanted to experience that for the first time and she thought if he could hit her G spot, she might get there. The minute her back hit the tile wall, she sucked in a ragged breath waiting for him to start to move.

"Better?" he asked, bringing her legs up over his forearms like before.

"Yeah." He moved his hips and she moaned low in her throat as he hit the right spot. "Oh hell yeah. Right there."

He slowly slid his cock in and out.

"Please."

"Harder?"

"Yes, please, I need—" He slammed into her with several pumps of his hips, sending her skyrocketing into a soul-shattering climax. "Jason!"

She no more came down from one as he said, "You can come again, darlin'. Play with your clit."

"I can't." She panted, feeling boneless as he continued to piston into her. Her body came alive even though she thought for sure she couldn't come again. With each of his thrusts hitting her G spot, her pussy clamped down like she wanted to.

"Yes you can. Play with your clit, baby. Come for me again."

"God, Jason."

"Come on, darlin'. You can do it."

He continued to drive her mad with want as he slowed his thrusts. She reached down between them to spread wetness around her clit and finger the tiny nub of nerves. She couldn't believe it, but she wanted to come so badly, she hurt. "You're driving me insane."

"Good. I don't want to be there by myself when my world implodes."

"Come with me."

"I'm right there. Are you?"

"Yeah, just a little—fuck!" Her climax hit her like a boulder rolling down a mountain to hit a brick wall. "God!"

Jason moaned in her ear as he shuddered to his own completion at the same time. His body shook beneath her fingers as he slipped out of her. After he let her legs fall to the floor, she smoothed her hands down his chest.

"We should shower."

"I would love to shower with you and then I can finish making us dinner. Dessert kind of came before the main course." He reached over and turned on the warm water for a minute before he flipped the showerhead on.

She grabbed the soap and began lathering it in her hands before slicking them over his pecs and abdomen.

The soap bubbles slithered down between his legs. She scooped up some, rubbing the slippery substance around his flaccid cock.

"Keep that up and we'll be having more dessert before dinner."

"You going to be up for more so soon?" she asked, rubbing the soap around his balls and the base of his cock, fascinated by the hardening flesh.

"Babe, I'm perpetually horny around you, but we need to eat before we do anything else." One of his sexy eyebrows went up over his eye. "Besides, I have more things I want to do to you."

"Oh?"

"Ever had anal sex?"

"No."

"Would you like to try it?"

She shrugged as she palmed his cock. "As long as there isn't soap involved, I'm game to experience new things."

He tipped his head back on his shoulders as a groan rumbled low in his chest. "I would love to show you all kinds of new things, but if you don't stop that, I'm going to blow again."

"Already?"

"Okay, stop." He pushed her hand away before he stepped under the spray of water to wash the soap off. "Your turn." With a palm full of soap, he washed her from neck to toes, spending a little more time than necessary on her breasts and pussy. "I need to make sure they are clean inside and out so I can feast on your willing flesh after dinner." He guided her under the water to wash all the suds away and then turned off the spigot. After he grabbed two towels to dry off, he pushed her with a hand on her butt toward the door.

"I think my clothes are in living room."

"That's okay. We can eat naked, or you can anyway."

"What if your family comes by?" she asked, with a giggle. "I'm sure you don't want to show off my assets to them."

He wrapped her up in his arms as he kissed her on the nose. "Hell no. I'm not sharing. I'm a pretty possessive guy when I like what I have."

"And do you like what you have?"

"You *are* mine."

"Am I? That sounded pretty possessive to me. I thought we weren't doing a relationship."

"I thought we were dating?"

He headed for the kitchen with just a towel around his hips, enticing her to tear the cotton material off and suck him dry. "Dating, yeah. Exclusive?"

With a glance over his shoulder, he said, "I don't share well." He opened the door on the oven to check whatever was inside. Apparently the food had been cooking on low while they were busy having wild sex.

"You've never been this way with any other woman, why me?"

"I like the way we are. I want it to continue."

"This sounds an awful lot like a relationship, Jason."

He grabbed a knife and began chopping some vegetables to put into a salad bowl. "So it's a relationship."

She popped one of the pieces of celery into her mouth. "I thought we weren't doing a relationship?"

"What's the problem?" he asked, pointing the knife in her direction. "I'm okay with this being what it is, but now you aren't?"

"I wasn't before. I know your reputation. This doesn't sound like you."

"So I'm evolving with what's going on between us. Isn't that okay? I thought things could change between two people."

He continued to chop, but his movements told her she was agitating him beyond words. "I'm sorry. I don't mean to question your motives, but you have to understand where I'm coming from. I've seen nothing from you up to this point, to indicate you were looking for something serious. Now you are changing your tune completely?"

When his movements paused, he turned to face her for a moment to say, "I don't know what I'm looking for, Peyton. All I know is I'm not letting you go if I don't have to. We're good together and I want it to continue until we decide otherwise."

She exhaled sharply as she headed back into the living room to put on her clothes. He might feel comfortable running around in nothing but a towel around his tempting hips, but she needed clothing.

Once she had everything on, she returned to the kitchen to find dinner almost ready and Jason dressed in a low slung pair of jeans. "What are we having?"

"Roasted chicken with mashed potatoes, salad and vegetables."

"Sounds good. Do you like to cook?"

"Yeah. I loved being in the kitchen with my mom while we were growing up. Not having any girls was hard on her, but I enjoyed helping her."

"Smells wonderful."

"Thanks. If you take a seat, I'll get it on the table in the dining room in a second. Everything is done." The apparent agitation he was feeling earlier must have resolved. He was back to his charming self as he placed the food on the table. "Help yourself. Would you like beer, wine, milk, water or what to drink?"

"I'll take a glass of wine."

"Red or white?"

"Aren't you supposed to have white with chicken?"

"I guess. I'm not a wine drinker. White it is." He returned a few minutes later with a glass half full of white wine and set it near the top of her plate. "Chardonnay?"

"Perfect. See? You know more about it than you think." She put her napkin on her lap and proceeded to cut into the chicken. The meat melted like butter on a hot sidewalk, on her tongue. "Wow. This is fabulous. I've never had chicken this tender and juicy before." His lips curved up in that sexy smile she'd come to think of as reserved for her.

"Thanks."

"How did you make it?"

"Several herbs, but the trick is to cook the chicken slowly on low heat so it doesn't dry out."

"Oh my gosh! This is absolutely amazing," she said around bites of the meat and potatoes. The man could really cook. "You'll have to cook for me all the time now that you've spoiled me on your cooking."

"Anytime, darlin'. I love someone who appreciates my *talents* in the kitchen."

She tilted her head slightly to the left and smiled. Oh she would definitely appreciate his talents in the kitchen over and over before the night was through, if she had her way about it.

Chapter Eleven

The conversation during dinner veered away from anything too serious. They talked about the ranch and his duties, his plans for his own herd as well as the bulls he was breeding for the PBR. Her plans for school coming up in the fall, although she didn't go into detail about why she wanted to be an abuse counselor. She didn't feel ready to tell him about Charles.

"When did you get your first piercing?"

"Do you mean besides my earlobes like every other little girl?"

"Yeah." He shoved his plate away and leaned back in his chair. "You have what, your tongue, your ears, belly button which is totally hot, by the way, your eyebrow. What else?"

"Nothing. That's it. Isn't it enough?"

"I guess. Which was your first besides your ears?"

"I did several holes in my ears before I did anything else. The rest came after."

"After what?"

She bit her lower lip as she tried to think of something to say that wouldn't go into the emotional abuse of her past. "After my belly button. I got that one next."

"Oh. Interesting. Is there a reason for each piercing?"

Fear slithered down her spine. She didn't want Jason to know of the emotional scars she still held deep in her soul. Charles certainly had done a number on her not only emotionally, but physically in the way she got the piercings to make her body fit into the picture perfect woman for him. Charles was a big burly man and although he never got physically abusive with her, the emotional toll was enough to send her into a tailspin. She could never please him—from sexual intercourse to cooking dinner—nothing was ever good enough for him. He belittled her constantly and when she'd try to stand up for herself, he'd deny there was a problem. She wanted to go to counseling then, but he refused, insisting there wasn't anything wrong with their relationship. Now that she knew more about emotional abuse, she understood the problem his constant verbal and emotional manipulation took on her. She didn't trust easily and that cumulated in her relationship with men.

"What do you mean?"

"Some people get tats to commemorate a loved one or something. I wasn't sure if the same thing applied to piercings."

For me, yes. I got each one in hopes of making myself beautiful for Charles. "No. I just felt like getting them." *I was never good enough for him.*

"Did they hurt? I mean tats kind of sting depending on where you get them, of course, but I've never had a piercing."

"Not really. They ache a little afterward for a while and you have to take good care of them, but otherwise, no they don't hurt much."

"Are you okay? You seemed kind of lost in thought while we were talking about this."

"I'm fine. I just don't like talking about them."

"Why?"

She jumped to her feet, rubbing her arms to calm the goose bumps flittering across her skin. "I just don't, okay? Please, just let it go."

He moved to her side, took her in his arms and rubbed his hands up and down her back. "It's okay, Peyton. We don't have to discuss them anymore, if you don't want to."

"Thank you," she whispered, snaking her arms around his waist to hold him closer. The solid wall of his chest gave her comfort where she never had any before. Talking about this always made her antsy even with the therapist. *I thought I was over this. Apparently not. I need to make an appointment with Jamie to talk. It's been a couple of weeks.* She pulled him in tighter to chase away the self-doubts. Jason liked her just the way she was. She didn't have to pretend to be anything with him, but the woman.

"Do you want to help me with dishes?"

She sniffed to hide the well of tears sure to break loose if he so much as kissed her right now. This man made everything in her life seem like it wasn't too bad after all. "Sure."

While they cleaned the kitchen, she didn't say much although she kept feeling Jason's gaze on her several times. "What?"

"Nothing. I'm just amazed you're here with me."

"Why?"

"Because you're a very beautiful woman. You could probably have any guy you wanted and you're here with me."

"Oh please. You're the playboy. You've got three quarters of the women over the age of eighteen all twittering like a bunch of thirteen year olds every time you come around. I've seen you at the bar, don't forget."

"You've been paying attention?"

"Yeah, for several months now."

"Interesting." He wrapped the towel he was using on the dishes, around her waist, dragging her into his embrace.

"What's so interesting?"

"You've been watching me."

"Why is that so thought-provoking?"

"Because I've been watching you. The way your hair shines beneath the lights of the bar. The way you grip a glass to pour a beer. How your hair caresses your cheek sometimes when it gets flipped in the front to rest on your breast." He punctuated each sentence with a kiss somewhere, her lips, her eyes, the shell of her ear, the slope of her neck, and the swell of her breast. "I've been dying to touch you for months now."

"You have?" She couldn't believe one of the most gorgeous men in Bandera had been interested in her for months while she panted after him like a lost puppy trying to find her master.

"Yeah."

He nipped at her bottom lip before he plunged his tongue between her parted lips to tangle with her own. *God, I love kissing this man.*

A knock sounded on the door and he groaned as he broke the kiss. "I'm going to kill whoever that is."

She giggled as she pushed him back by the shoulders. "We have all night."

"But I was just getting into kissing you."

"Me too."

The knock sounded again as he heard Jeff's voice outside the door. "Jason? Open up. There's a problem."

Jason sighed as he tipped his head back on his shoulders. "All right. I'm coming."

When he opened the door, Jeff pushed his way inside giving her a perfunctory glance as he turned to face his brother. "There's been an accident."

"What? Who?"

"Joel. Nothing serious, I don't think, but he's been taken to the hospital in San Antonio by ambulance. You coming?"

He raked his fingers through his hair. "Uh, yeah. Let me throw some clothes on."

Jeff glanced back at her, tipped his hat and headed back out the door. "I'll see you there."

"Yeah. I'll be right behind you." He stopped his frantic search for his clothes for a moment to take her in his arms. "I'm sorry."

"Don't be. You're family needs you. Go."

"You'll be here when I get back?"

"I don't think so."

With her hands clasped in his, he said, "Then go with me. I need you."

"Are you sure? I'll just be in the way."

"No you won't. Please?"

"All right. Let me put my boots on and comb my hair. I wouldn't want to show up at the hospital with sex hair." She shoved her fingers through the messy strands in an attempt to tame the wild mass.

He kissed her palms before he shoved a curl behind her ear. "I think you look damned sexy with it all mussed like that."

"That's your opinion, mister. Somehow I think your family is going to know what we were doing before Jeff got here."

He shrugged and stepped back. "Who cares. I don't."

She rolled her eyes as she moved to grab her boots from near the door and shoved her feet inside. Her purse lay on the bench so she grabbed it to find her brush. After running it through her hair a few times, she announced she was ready to go.

"We'll take my truck," he said, returning from putting his shirt and socks on that they'd discarded in the living room before their romp in the kitchen.

"You dressed pretty fast."

"I'm quick when I need to be."

"Not during sex, I hope."

He looked aghast as she laughed. "Never during sex."

They walked out to his truck, avoiding the dog who lounged on the porch, barely lifting his head when they walked around him. The night's inky black sky reflected a thousand stars twinkling overhead. No moon shone tonight to light their way, but she didn't care. She was with a guy she quickly realized her feelings went a lot deeper for than she wanted to admit. Her heart wasn't listening to her head and she was afraid her heart might win the argument.

* * * *

"What the hell did you do to yourself, Trip?" Jason asked Joel as they walked into emergency room at the local hospital. His nickname for his triplet siblings coming through loud and clear. He called Joel, Trip for triplet and Joshua, Doub for double. Jason's nickname from the family had always been One because he was the eldest of the three of them, then Joshua and last came Joel.

"Hit a damned deer with my truck." Joel glanced at his wife sitting next to him holding his hand. "Broke my leg in the process."

"You're lucky you didn't break your head open, you dumbshit."

"Like I had control, you asshole. I didn't plan on hitting a deer. It jumped out in front of me. I didn't have a chance to even stop before it was on my hood and half through my windshield. I'm just glad Mesa wasn't in the truck with me. The deer went into the passenger side seat practically." Joel kissed her fingertips. "I wouldn't want you hurt for anything."

Joshua gagged from his place in the corner. The bed had been completely surrounded by Young family members.

"It'll be your turn soon enough," Nina said, glancing at Jason's hand joined with Peyton's as they stood next to the bed with everyone else. "I'm glad this wasn't worse than it is. A broken leg can be managed although you won't be able to ride for a bit. Maybe you can take over doing some of the office stuff for me."

Joel blanched as Mesa laughed. "Yeah, I can see that. Joel behind a desk?"

"Well, what else is he going to do while he's in a cast for six to eight weeks?" Nina moved to where she stood near the head of Joel's bed. "You'll have to suck it up, buttercup."

The entire family laughed until the doctor came in through the curtains with a soft, "Whoa. Okay. I didn't realize the whole family would be here."

"He's one of ours, so yeah, you get all of us," Jeff replied from his spot near the sink. Terri must have stayed home with the boys since their little one wasn't very old yet.

Jason also noticed Paige wasn't there either, but then again with her twin pregnancy moving along at a rapid pace, she probably didn't need to be out here either. *Since when did I become such a mother hen with the women of our family?* He tucked Peyton's hand into the crook of his arm. "How are you feeling, bro?"

"Hurts like hell, but they've given me pain medicine."

"That's right and we'll be taking him to surgery soon," the doctor added, looking at the chart in his hand. "He'll need a plate or two to stabilize the break. It's a pretty bad fracture since the dashboard was shoved up into his lap. I'm surprised both legs aren't broken."

"Surgery?" Mesa asked, her grip tightening on Joel's hand.

"Yes. It's a must."

"Don't worry, baby. I'll be fine."

"You'd better be. We have some planning to do."

"I know, darlin'."

"Planning?" Nina asked, hope shining in her eyes.

"We didn't want to announce it this way, but we are expecting a baby in about eight months."

"Another grandchild!" Nina clapped before she bent over Joel, kissing him on the head and then doing the same with Mesa. "It's about time. You two have been together for a while."

"It's hasn't been that long, Mom."

"Long enough to expect a grandchild."

Joel and Mesa both laughed as they shook their heads.

Jason shook his brother's hand excitedly. He wasn't sure he wanted kids of his own, certainly not yet, but he was happy for his brother who he knew wanted several children. Mesa had been such a good thing for Joel when they'd gotten together even though when the whole thing started, Jason wasn't sure she was the right girl. The day they'd been married was a joyful occasion at the ranch and one he wouldn't forget.

"Well since everything is fine here, I'm going to head back home."

"You aren't staying for the surgery," James asked from his spot near the wall.

"Do I need to?"

"Had plans, did you?" Joel asked, eyeing Peyton as she stood near his right side. "Sorry I interrupted things."

"It's fine now that I know you're going to be okay. I couldn't have my brother coming to the hospital and me not seeing how you are even if it's nothing major."

"It could have been," Jeff said.

"I know, Jeff. That's why I came. He's still family even though he's my squirt of a younger brother."

"By fifteen minutes, for God's sake!"

"Still younger."

"Asshole."

"You'll be fine if you're cussing me out."

The nurse came through the curtain. "Everyone is going to have to clear out. I need to prep him for surgery, get another IV started and draw more blood."

"Damn woman. You already took two tubes."

"Suck it up. I need five more before they take you to surgery, plus the anesthesiologist will be coming in soon to talk to you."

"We're gone then," Jason said, moving toward the curtain. "Are they going to keep him for a couple of days afterward?"

"At least tomorrow, yes."

"I'll be back by in the morning then."

"Thanks for coming, Jason. I know you were busy with Peyton. I didn't mean to ruin your plans."

"It's okay. No problem. We were done with dinner already anyway so we're going to, ahem, watch a movie."

Joel's eyebrow shot up over his eye. "Movie?"

"Yeah, a movie. Right Peyton?"

"What movie?" The whole group laughed as she blushed so hard the roots of her hair turned red too.

"Come on, babe. Let's go home."

Nina grinned as they all walked out of the curtained area and back down the hall toward the waiting room. The rest of the family left, leaving Jason, Peyton and his mother and father. Mesa, of course, stayed at her husband's bedside until they wheeled him out toward the operating room. Then she joined his parents to wait.

"He'll be fine." Jason hugged Mesa. "I know he will."

"I know, but I'm worried. What if something happens? What if he goes into cardiac arrest or what if he has a reaction to the anesthesia?"

"Is there any reason to worry? No. Quit freaking yourself out."

"I know. I'm being silly, but I love him so much and now that there is a baby on the way, I don't know what I'd do without him."

Nina put her arms around Mesa, cradling her almost like a lost child. Jason felt out of touch with the whole scenario even though it was his triplet brother in there. They didn't talk about it much, but the three of them had a bond. When one hurt, the others hurt. When one was sad, the others could feel it and when Joel had fallen hard for Mesa, Jason knew in his heart she was perfect for his brother in the end.

"We are headed out. Call me when he's out of surgery, please, or I won't sleep a wink tonight and I'll be back up here before morning."

"Of course, son," his dad answered before his mother could as she stood there rocking Mesa and whispering to her that Joel would be fine.

Jason put his arm around Peyton as they walked toward the door. "Thanks, Dad. See you at home."

The ride back to his house was made in silence as he contemplated the turn of events for his brother, his triplet. Joel was going to be a daddy himself and man did it make Jason feel old. His younger sibling was married with a baby on the way. Wasn't it time he settled down too? He glanced across the truck at Peyton. Was she the one? Should he give up his wandering ways for the love of one woman? What if she didn't love him? What if she cheated on him? What if she didn't want anything more than sex like they'd talked about in the beginning? Did he want more now?

"What are you thinking about?" she asked, cocking her head to the side.

"Lots of things."

"Like?"

"What if I asked you to marry me?"

"What? Are you nuts?"

"Maybe am I. I'm thinking about my future and I think you'd be a good fit."

"I'm not marrying you, Jason."

"Why not?"

"We've been dating for what? Two weeks and you want me to marry you? You're crazy."

"No I'm not. My brother did it. He seems happy. I want that too."

"Not with me, you don't."

"Sure I do. You'd be as good as any, I'm thinking."

She punched him in the shoulder. "As good as any? You ask me to marry you without even professing to love me and I'm as good as any? Why don't you just go to The Dusty Boot, grab the first woman who walks through the door and ask her? It'd be about as romantic and caring as the proposal I just got."

"Now just wait a minute, Peyton. I mean we get along good. We're good in bed together. We seem to have some things in common. You're pretty enough."

"Thanks, for that, but no. Take your proposal and stuff it up your ass."

They pulled into the driveway in front of his house. The truck hadn't even come to a complete halt and she was out the passenger side door headed for her car.

"What the hell? Where are you going?" he asked, rushing around the front of his truck as the headlights reflected off the porch. He grabbed the door to her car before she could shut it.

"Let go."

"No, let's talk about this."

"There isn't anything to talk about. I'm not marrying you."

"Fine. Then let's keep going the way we are."

"You know, I don't think so. You want something I can't give you apparently. You've changed, Jason. You said you didn't want a wife and I was good with that since I didn't want to be a wife, but now you're asking me to marry you out of the blue."

"Come inside."

"No. I'm going home. I don't want to see you anymore. We obviously want different things in this." She waved her hand back and forth. "Whatever this is."

"Don't go, Peyton."

"We're done, Jason. I'm sorry, but this isn't going to work." She slammed the door shut, started the car and then backed out of his life in a spray of gravel.

Chapter Twelve

Jason twirled the rope he held over his head before tossing it expertly over the horns of the bull he intended to move to the barn. He had some cows he needed to inseminate. The work on a ranch never ended, never took a break nor did it stop for a broken heart.

Broken heart, bah!

Joshua helped herd the bull through the panels to the holding pen Jason had fashioned so he could collect the sperm from the bull. The steer he planned to use to get the bull ready was already in place. Joey stood nearby waiting with the ejaculation kit for when the bull mounted the steer. Joshua threaded another rope through the ring on the bull's nose as Jason dismounted from his horse and removed the one around the animal's neck. "I'll take it from here." He took the ejaculation kit from Joey as the bull jumped to mount the steer. He easily got the false vagina on the bull, capturing the bull's semen. "See. Easy as pie."

"Do you know which of your cattle you're going to inseminate and your schedule?" Joey asked. He usually handled the horses on their parent's place, but today, Jacob manned the horses and took the guests out. Jacob needed to stay close these days as Paige could have the babies at any time.

"Yeah. Got them penned in the other side of the barn already waiting."

"Perfect," Joshua said, releasing the rope on the bull's nose ring so they didn't tear it out by accident.

The nose ring helped to control the bull during the ejaculation process.

This bull was Jason's prized possession and his ace in the hole for having prime livestock for the PBR in the coming years ahead.

"How are things with Peyton?" Joey asked, moving the steer they'd use for bait.

"Who?" Jason didn't want to talk about how shit had gone down with her. He didn't want to talk about her, didn't want to think about her and certainly didn't want to tell his brothers he'd fucked up royally by asking her to marry him in a nervous fuck up.

"Peyton? You know. Pretty, nice rack, works at The Dusty Boot? I thought you were fucking her?" The look in Joshua's eyes as he brought up Peyton made Jason want to punch him.

"I was. Drop it."

"Ah." Joshua and Joey exchanged amused glances.

"Quit acting like you two are laughing."

"We aren't laughing at you, Jason. We're laughing with you. I bet she was a great lay."

"Maybe, but it's none of your business anyway."

"If you aren't fucking her anymore, you can tell us." The brothers leaned over the metal fencing with their arms under their chins.

"Yeah, spill it," Joey said, his eyes gleaming with curiosity.

"I don't fuck and gossip."

The two brothers looked at each other and then back at him. "Sure you do. You always have before, what's so special about her?" Joshua asked, putting the toe of his cowboy boot on the bottom rung of the fence in preparation for a longwinded discussion about women.

"I'm not talking to you about Peyton."

"Why not? What's the deal?"

Jason stored the sperm in a container to inseminate the cows in a little while. He needed to take care of the bull and the steer first. He wiped down his hands with disinfectant. "Because I don't. What happened between us is private."

"I don't believe you. You always talk about the women you've been with." Joshua elbowed Joey. "Didn't he talk about, what was her name? Sheila?"

"Oh don't get me started on her. She's trying to say she's pregnant with my child."

"She what?" Joshua asked, shock clearly written on his face. "Didn't you use a condom man?"

"After we'd been together a few times, no. She said she was on birth control."

"And you fell for that shit?" Joey shook his head. "Never fall for that crap. She's a user if I ever saw one."

"I know. Right now I'm not even sure she's really pregnant, much less if it's mine. I know she's been with other guys since me so who knows." Jason grabbed the rope to lead the bull back outside into the holding pen he would be housed in until they'd extracted a few more sperm samples from him.

"What did Peyton say?"

"What the hell does it matter? Peyton and I aren't together anymore so let it go."

"What happened between you two? You seemed happy before, now you're like a bear with a thorn in its paw," Joey said, lifting his hat off his head and wiping his brow from the sweat collecting under the brim.

The heat today was almost unbearable especially in the stuffiness of the barn. Sunlight filtered through the hayloft slats to the floor below, reflecting the dust floating in the air. The bull stomped his feet, stirring up the dirt from beneath his hoofs as Jason got him situated in his pen. "Easy boy. You'll get your treats and feed in a minute."

"Yeah, Jason. Tells us what happened."

He shut the gate behind the bull. "I asked her to marry me."

"What? Seriously?" Joshua slapped him on the back. "I guess since you aren't seeing each other anymore, she said no."

"Not just no, but hell no."

"Why'd you do something so stupid?" Joey stood with his hands on his hips and his legs braced apart like he planned to jump on some bucking bronc to bring him to his knees.

"God love you, little brother. I really hadn't figured out how stupid I was before now."

"Well?"

He shrugged as he coiled the rope he'd been using. "I don't know why I asked her. After what happened with Joel and realizing all of this could be gone in a split second, I thought about having someone permanent in my life instead of fucking anything that moved. I really want that for some unfucking godly reason."

"With Peyton?" Joshua asked, his stunned expression almost hilarious.

Jason laughed as he nodded his head. "Yeah, with Peyton."

Joshua nodded, clapping Jason on the back. "Good for you, brother. I can see you two together. She seems like a nice girl."

"Wait. Did you miss the part where we aren't seeing each other anymore? She turned me down flat right before she sprayed dust and gravel all over my front door in a hurry to get out of my life."

"You'll convince her."

"And just how the hell am I supposed to do that? She won't even talk to me. I've tried. I've sent her text message after text message. I never get a reply."

"Have you lost what little sense Mom and Dad gave you?" Joey asked. "You don't do this kind of shit over text message, you dumbass. Go to her house. Corner her. Fuck her. Talk to her. Whatever. If you really want her, you need to get right in her face and make her listen to you."

"Oh and you're an expert on relationships? You don't even have a girlfriend."

"But if I did, I'd know how to treat her. I would make sure she knew she was the most important thing in my life the whole time we are together. I'd bring her roses. Take her to lunch just because. Buy her special little presents. You know, all those things girls like."

Jason rubbed his chin, the whisker scraping against his palm. He hadn't shaved in a couple of days, hoping he'd have a chance to talk to Peyton. He thought she liked the five o'clock shadow and rough whisker burn on her skin. He knew he liked seeing it on her. "Maybe."

"Maybe? You really need to pull your head out of your ass, brother. Do you want her?"

"Yes."

"No, do you really want her, like as in permanently?"

"I think so. I mean I can't picture my bed or my life without her in it these days."

"Then go to her."

"Okay. I will. After we're done with this shit this afternoon. I'll go to her house and make her listen to me so she'll realize, I was a bit desperate when I asked her to marry me and maybe that is in the cards down the road, but we can go back to what we had before I blurted that out."

"There you go!" Joshua punched him in the arm. "Now you're on the right track."

"I'm not sure I am, but what do I have to lose. She won't talk to me now so it can't hurt anything by going over there unless she's got a shotgun or something."

* * * *

Peyton stared at the television without conscious thought of what actually played in front of her face.

Paige swiped her hand in front of Peyton's eyes. "Where are you?"

"Huh?"

"You are totally not here right now."

"Sorry. I know we are supposed to be having a girl's night out, but I'm not into this." Peyton got to her feet, spilling popcorn from the bowl as she sat it down on the coffee table. "My mind is elsewhere."

"Yeah, we know," Mandy said, picking up the popcorn bowl.

Her phone beeped. Another text message. She knew who it was from without even looking. Jason. He just didn't give up although he didn't bug her at the bar or come by her house, he still sent text message after text message trying to get her to talk to him. At the bar, he watched her, unnerving her to no end with his piercing blue eyes. He always stayed until she closed, never leaving until he knew she was safely in her car. It had kind of become a game to her. See how pissed off she could make him by flirting with guys at the bar, but she never went home with any of them. No, Jason Young had wormed his way into her thoughts, dreams and life inside of a few short weeks. *Damn him.*

Being this hung up on a guy usually turned out bad. Look at her relationship with Charles.

"Honey, what's wrong?" Paige asked, grimacing a little as she shifted on the couch.

"Are you okay?"

"Yeah, my back hurts is all. Nothing new there, but it's been cramping off and on all day."

"Cramping? Are you sure you aren't in labor, Paige?"

Paige cocked her head to the side. "I still have like two weeks before they'll even take them c-section. I can't be in labor."

"Paige, you're having twins. They do whatever the hell they want. I think you should go to the hospital to get checked out."

"Really?"

"Yeah, really."

"I need to call Jacob. Can you drive me? I'm scared."

"Nothing to be scared about. Those babies are well done already. Aren't you like thirty-eight weeks?"

"Yeah, but I thought pregnancy lasted forty weeks?"

"In the perfect world, honey, but with twins, it's not unusual to have them early." Peyton grabbed her tennis shoes and slipped them on in a rush. Who cared if she was in her Hello Kitty pajama bottoms, a T-shirt and shoes with no socks? Her friend needed her. "You can call Jacob from the car. Let's go."

She quickly ushered Paige and Mandy out to her car, got them inside as Paige got on the phone with Jacob, and then went around to the driver's side. It was going to be a long night if Paige was in labor.

"Hi Honey. Yeah, it's me. Listen, Peyton is taking me to the hospital. I've been cramping all day. I know. It's okay. No, my water hasn't broke. It'll be okay, Jacob. I'm in good hands. Just meet us at the hospital in the labor and delivery department. We'll be there in about forty-five minutes depending on how fast Peyton drives." She glanced at Peyton as she nodded. "Yeah, forty-five minutes. Okay. I love you. See you soon."

Peyton took her hand and squeezed her fingers. "You'll be fine."

"I know. I trust you."

"Thanks. We'll get there in plenty of time."

Twenty minutes later, found them on the side of the road changing a tire. "Fuck, fuck, fuck!"

"Is this going to take much longer, Peyton? I think it's definitely labor. My belly is cramping now."

"How far apart?"

"About five minutes."

"Shit. I'll hurry."

"I sure don't want to have these babies in your car."

"I don't want you to either."

Headlights blinded her for a moment as a truck pulled up behind her car before it shut off. "Oh, thank you, Lord. I hope it's someone who can change this damned tire faster or take Paige onto the hospital before it's too late."

"Peyton?"

"Ah, fuck. It had to be Jason," she mumbled under her breath.

"Jacob has half the county searching for you guys. What's the problem?"

"I picked up a nail and got a flat. I can't get these damned lug nuts off. They are too tight."

"Let me try."

He crouched down beside her, bringing the scent of his aftershave with him. That smell on him did wild things to her insides. She inhaled, bringing the scent to her nose as she closed her eyes.

"Are you sniffing me?"

She caught herself leaning toward him with a jerk. "No."

A half crooked smile creased his lips while he wrestled the last of the lug nuts loose. *Damn the man.*

"Grab the spare for me, would you, please? We'll get you ladies on the road here in a minute."

Within minutes, he had the tire changed.

"Can you hurry please?" Paige groaned as another pain hit her. "They are pretty close together."

"We'll be on our way in a second. Hang tight." She glanced at Jason as they both stood and he put the tire back in the trunk. "Thank you."

"You're welcome. Get her to the hospital before she has those babies in your car."

"We aren't far. Five minutes."

"Hit the emergency room when you get there. Jacob has everyone on high alert."

"Will do." She saluted smartly before she walked around to slide inside the car. Jason stood by his truck as she pulled away, watching him in the rearview mirror. She wondered if he'd follow to the hospital since Jacob sent him out looking for them. Sure enough, he pulled out behind them, the lights of his truck reflecting in her eyes as she glanced back, keeping him in sight.

Thirty minutes later, they pulled into the overhang of the emergency room. Two nurses with a wheelchair rushed out and around to the passenger side of the car as Peyton and Mandy got out. "She's having pains about three minutes apart."

"We'll take it from here." As one nurse helped Paige out of the car, water gushed down her legs. "It appears your water just broke. We are taking you straight to the delivery room. We can check you there."

"But they were supposed to be born by c-section, not natural."

"Honey, these babies decide when they're coming and how they're coming, we don't. You'll do fine."

"Where's Jacob?"

"Right here, darlin'," Jacob answered coming around the car. "What happened to you and Peyton? I thought I would go crazy."

"We got a flat. I couldn't get the damned lug nuts off."

"Jacob, I'm scared."

"You'll be fine, baby. Let's get you inside. The doctor is waiting."

"Oh." She held her stomach as she doubled over in pain.

"Get her inside. I have a feeling baby number one will be making his or her debut soon," the nurse said, taking control of the situation as they pushed her inside the double doors.

Peyton stood there, not sure what to do next. Her friend was in good hands, she hoped, and the babies would be born without any complications. She had to believe that.

"Pull your car around to the parking lot and park to the side. You can meet her upstairs," the second nurse said before she went through the double doors behind Paige.

After a few seconds, Peyton got back in the car with Mandy in the front passenger seat and moved her car to an empty spot. She debated for a few moments when she saw one available next to Jason's truck. He wasn't in it. Apparently, he'd already gone inside to let Jacob know they'd arrived. Good. She really didn't want to be near him anymore than she had to. Not that she minded his physical nearness, but being too close to him brought back the memories she'd been trying desperately to forget over the last two weeks. "Marry him. Is he crazy?"

"What'd you'd say? Marry who?"

"Jason."

"What? He asked you to marry him?"

"Yeah, crazy, huh?"

"I would have said yes in a heartbeat."

Peyton opened her door and slammed it shut behind her as Mandy got out on the other side. "Well, I didn't. I told him he was nuts and there would be no way I would marry him now or any time in the near future. We fucked. It was good, but I'm not in love with him."

"I think you protest too much myself. If you really thought about it for more than a few minutes, you'd realize you are at least half in love with the man already." Mandy came around the front of the car.

"You're as crazy as he is, Mandy." Peyton headed for the sliding door to the hospital lobbying. Bah, in love with Jason. No way. She wouldn't give into that silly emotion especially with a cowboy. Yeah, he was good in bed. They connected that way, but really what else did they have in common? He came from a prominent, solid *large* family whereas she came from a nonexistent one.

She had baggage, emotional scars she wasn't sure she could get past with another man. Fucking had been great between them, but she didn't do emotion very well with anyone. Not since Charles raked her through the coals with breaking her down to a needy wreck.

"You need to move on, Peyton. Jason is a good guy."

"Move on from what?"

"I know about Charles."

"How? I never told you."

Mandy put an arm around Peyton's shoulders even though she tried to shake her off. "Yes you did. One night, when you were very drunk, you broke down and told me everything. He did a number on you, I'll give you that, but are you going to let him ruin you for any other man?"

"Butt out."

"I can't. You are my friend. I see how miserable you are. You were happy when you were with Jason, you aren't now. You've been a bitch the last two weeks since you walked out on him."

"I can handle my relationship with Jason."

"You don't have a relationship, remember?"

"I don't want one either."

"You might lie to me. You might lie to Jason, but don't lie to yourself. You're the only one who knows everything about what is going on inside your brain and your heart. He's good for you. Admit it, even if it's only to yourself." Mandy kissed her on the cheek before she walked inside the hospital, leaving Peyton to ponder her words as she watched from outside.

Jason stood with his family in the waiting room. Every Young was there except Joel, Mesa and Terri who probably stayed home with the boys since they wouldn't be allowed in the hospital anyway. It wasn't a good idea to have kids around all those germs. They looked happy awaiting the arrival of the newest additions to the family.

When Mandy walked in, Jason greeted her with a smile. Jealousy zinged through Peyton. Was he flirting with Mandy? Did Mandy flirt back? Was there something going on there between them? Maybe he'd been fucking all of them simultaneously. Her, Mandy, and Sheila.

"No, that's nuts. I would have known."

Would you?

Jason broke off from the crowd and came out the doors toward her. "Hi."

"Hi."

"You okay?" he asked, shoving his hands in the front pocket of his jeans.

"Yeah."

"Why are you standing out here?

"Just gettin' some air."

"You can come in with the family, you know. You're good friends with Paige. No one will kick you out."

"I didn't think they would, but…"

"But what, Peyton? Is it me?"

"Well, it's kind of awkward, you know, since we were doing the horizontal mambo."

He smiled as he looked down at the toes of his boots. "Sorry."

"It's okay." She frowned.

"What's the frown for?"

"Something Mandy told me before she went inside is bugging me."

"Something you want to talk about?"

"Not with you."

"Is it about me?"

"Yeah. She's wrong, but you know, it's kind of stuck in my brain and I need to work it out."

"I miss you, you know."

"Please don't."

"Why? It's the truth. I still think about your body pressed up against mine, the warmth of your pussy around my cock when we were making love."

"Fucking, Jason. We were fucking."

"Whatever you want to call it to justify everything in your mind, you go right ahead, darlin', but to me, we were making love."

Chapter Thirteen

Jason scuffed the toe of his boot at a rock, dislodging the stone as he sent it across the grass. "I know I sent you into a tailspin with the marriage thing."

"You think so?"

"Yeah, I know so, but listen. I'm sorry. I was kind of thinking weird the day Joel got hurt and realizing how fast things can change. Not that I didn't mean it."

She put up her hand. "Don't, Jason. I'm not marrying you."

"I'm not asking you to. I just want us to date again."

"Why?"

He skimmed a finger down her cheek. "I miss you. I said that already, but it's true."

Her body broke out in goose bumps from her head to her toes as a shiver rolled through her.

"And I think you miss me too."

"Whatever gave you that idea?"

"Your reaction right now. Don't tell me my touch doesn't affect you because I know it does, just like yours affects me."

"I don't know what you're talkin' about."

"Liar," he whispered, his mouth near her ear. "Are you wet? I'm hard as a damned brick just thinking about you all warm around me."

"Jason, please."

"Please what? Please make love to you? Please, kiss you? Please, touch you where you burn for me?"

Joshua popped his head out the door. "Hey, Jase. The babies are here."

"I'll be right there." He stepped back, taking his heat with him. "This isn't over."

With her hand in his, he led her inside to find out about the babies Paige just gave birth to. Peyton's mind whirled with emotions, sensations and confusion. She didn't know how she felt about Jason these days, but she would have to figure things out soon or go mad trying.

When they made it inside, the way Nina's eyebrow shot up over her eye seeing Peyton's hand clasped tightly in Jason's left her nervous. Nina smiled as she nodded so she figured it would be okay to leave it there...for now.

"It's a boy and a girl!" Jacob shouted as he came out of the obstetrics ward where they'd all moved after Jason and Peyton joined them. "They are healthy and screaming their lungs out. Paige is tired, but fine."

"My first granddaughter!" Nina asked, tears rolling down her cheeks as she hugged Jacob to her. "Names?"

"We haven't decided yet, but you'll be the first to know, Mom."

"Congratulations, son." James slapped him on the back. "Go be with your wife and children. We'll take it from here."

Peyton felt tears welling up in her own eyes as she thought about how far Paige and Jacob had come in such a short time. They hadn't been married long after Paige found out about her pregnancy, but they seemed happy together and very much in love.

How do I feel about finding someone to love for the rest of my life?

"You okay?"

"Yeah." She fanned her hands in front of her face, trying desperately to dry the tears. "Just a little teary thinking about those babies' parents. Theirs is such a great love story."

"It sure is. Did you see the first time they met?"

"Yes. I was working the bar that night. Dan tried to get her to stay out of it, but she couldn't. Not Paige. She is always one for the underdog."

"And now they are a happy family with two little ones."

"She's going to make a great mom."

"Jacob will make a great dad too. He's always loved kids."

"What about you? Do you want kids someday?"

"Maybe, but not for quite a while. I'd like to be just a couple for a few years to spend time with my woman." He dropped his arm around her shoulders.

Jacob came back out the doors. "Two can go in at a time to see Paige. The babies are in the nursery getting cleaned up, weighed and measured right at the moment."

"Peyton, why don't you and Jason go in first? I know you all want to get home soon."

"Thanks, Nina."

Peyton walked up and kissed Jacob on the cheek. "Congrats, Daddy."

He grinned so wide, she thought maybe his face would crack as he puffed up his chest and repeated, "Daddy. I like the sound of that."

When the two of them followed him back, they went by the nursery first to take a peek at the babies. Both were wrapped really tightly in a little blue blanket and a little pink blanket with matching knit hats.

"Aren't they gorgeous?" Jacob asked, tapping on the window as the nurse brought the little boy closer. "I haven't any idea what we are going to name them."

"You two didn't discuss names?"

"Oh, we did, but we couldn't agree. I think I want to name them after Paige's parents though since they aren't here to see their grandchildren."

"How sweet of you, Jacob. I'm sure she'd love it."

"We'll see. She's pretty emotional right now."

"Well, duh. She just gave birth. She's going to be emotional for a while."

"Shit. Really? She's been such a mess for so long during this pregnancy, I was hoping it would all magically go away when the babies were born."

"Don't count on it for about six weeks. It'll take that long for her body to get back to some semblance of normal."

"What about sex?"

"Six weeks, buddy," Jason said, grinning.

"I hate you."

"Don't blame me, blame the doctor. Maybe she won't make you wait that long."

"God, I hope not."

Peyton laughed as they walked down the corridor to the room Paige was in. When they pushed open the door and peeked inside, she was lying on the bed dressed in her pretty pajamas she'd packed in her bag, resting.

"Is she asleep?"

"No, she's not asleep," Paige answered, opening her eyes. "Hey. Come in. Did you see the babies?"

"They were taking the little girl for a bath so we didn't get a close look at her, but we saw your son. What a handsome devil he's going to be."

"I know, right?"

"How are you feeling?"

"Like I've been hit by a bus, but thanks for asking."

"I'm sorry things go so screwed up."

Paige squeezed her hand. "We made it. That's all that matters, although we might not have had Jason not found us and changed the tire."

"You look ravishing, Paige." He leaned over to kiss her forehead.

"Oh stop with you and the flattery, brother-in-law. I look like shit dried up in the summer Texas sun, rolled and boiled to a crisp."

They all laughed. "We won't stay long. There is a ton of people out there waiting to see you and those gorgeous babies. I just wanted to say congratulations. I'll come by to visit tomorrow when things calm down. I want my cuddle time with the twins."

"There will be plenty of that to go around although with having the first granddaughter, I think you might be fighting Nina for cuddle time."

"Well, I have to give her first dibs since she is their grandmother, but as their godmother, I get them second." Peyton smiled as she patted Paige's hand. "Rest. I'll see you tomorrow."

"Okay. Thanks again for everything."

"You're welcome."

"Oh, and I'll expect the gossip when you come tomorrow."

"Gossip?"

Paige tilted her head noting Jason standing close to Peyton.

"Nothing to tell."

"Uh-uh." Paige shook her head. "You can't fool me."

Peyton stepped back. "We'll be going now."

"See you tomorrow."

Jason took her hand as they walked out of the room. She glanced back at Paige, noticing how her eyes twinkled when she caught the gesture. There would be no living with her come tomorrow when she visited. She better think of something fast or Paige would have her and Jason married off in the next couple of weeks.

* * * *

Jason walked Peyton out to her car after Mandy had a chance to visit briefly with Paige as well. He knew he couldn't let her go. If he did, he might never see her again and that wasn't acceptable to him. The need for her drove him to distraction. He couldn't think. He couldn't sleep. He couldn't eat. He was a mess all the way around without her and he would just have to convince her she belonged with him until he could come to terms with this need he harbored for her. He stopped with her next to the car.

"Come home with me."

"You can't be serious," she whispered, trying not to let Mandy know what he said. "I'm not going home with you."

"Why not?"

"We aren't seeing each other at the moment."

"But I want you."

"This is crazy, Jason. You can't just take me home."

"I don't understand what the problem is. When we were having sex before, you didn't have a problem with just coming home with me at the bonfire."

"I know, but that was different."

"Different how?"

She exhaled sharply as she rolled her eyes. "Just different. Besides, I have Mandy with me. We were having a girl's night when Paige went into labor."

"Oh."

"Yeah, oh. I can't just dump her off, tell her to go home, and then come over to your place."

"How about tomorrow?"

"I think I need to do some serious deliberating before I decide to sleep with you again. I'm not sure us getting involved is a good idea."

"We need to talk about it."

"You don't talk. You touch, kiss, nibble, bite…"

"I know. It's amazing, huh?"

"You're lack of communication on this matter is increasingly disturbing." She sighed as he brushed his lips over the curve of her neck.

"I'm trying to communicate my need."

"Your *need* is very apparent against my abdomen."

"See. I'm communicating."

"You are, too much."

They both jumped as Mandy honked the horn on the car. "Get it on or let's go. I'm tired of waitin'."

"I'll call you tomorrow since you've been ignoring my text messages."

"I wasn't interested."

"Are you now?"

"Maybe, but I need a couple of days to think things through, Jason."

He brushed his knuckled over the protruding tip of her breast, stopping her breath in her throat. "No thinking. Just feel."

"I'm feeling a little overwhelmed with you right now."

A deep sigh escaped his lips as he stepped back. "All right. I'll leave you alone. But don't think you can ignore me."

"I won't. You're a pretty persistent guy."

He grinned as he noticed how the flood light from the parking lot of the hospital shone on her face. Her eyes sparkled with interest. Her body called to him to throw her up on the hood of her car and fuck the daylights out of her, but not here. He wanted their reunion to be special, soft, inviting, with candles and soft music playing in the background. Maybe a bubble bath for two. He could be romantic when the need arose.

"Let me call you when I've had time to think."

"Two days, Peyton. I'm giving you two days. If I don't hear from you by then, I'm coming after you." He crushed his mouth against hers, tasting her like he'd die if he did get enough of her soon. The last two weeks had been hell on him, wishing for her to be near, wanting her, dreaming of her, and all the while not wanting to rush her. Well to hell with that, he was done giving her space.

Her hands went up around his neck as she pushed her breasts against his chest. Their kiss lasted a lifetime, but wasn't long enough when he finally lifted his head to look deep into her eyes. Yes, she wanted him, but fear mixed with confusion reflected in her gaze.

"I'll talk to you soon."

"Okay. Be safe going home."

"I will. You too."

She slipped inside her car and shut the door before he watched her back up. Red taillights reflected the slow drizzle beginning to wet the pavement. Summer rain. It would wash the dirt, grime and evil out of the air, leaving things fresh and clean. He dipped his head as he headed back inside to say goodbye to his family before heading home.

His parents were inside visiting Paige and the babies so he talked to the brothers standing nearby, told them he'd see them at home and then headed out to his truck. He needed time to plan the re-seduction of Peyton Matthews.

* * * *

Two days had passed and she still wasn't any closer to coming to a conclusion about Jason. She liked him, liked him a lot, but did she want to try some relationship with him? She still didn't know. What about the emotional scars of Charles' reign?

"So how are you feeling these days?" her therapist asked as she sat down in the chair in her office.

"Good. Physically, anyway. Emotionally, I'm not so sure."

"Why? What's going on?"

"There's this guy."

"Isn't there always a guy who is a bane of our problems?"

She laughed, the sound coming from her mouth hollow and without emotion. "Seems so."

"So tell me about this guy."

"He's sweet, gorgeous, about six-four, muscular and a cowboy."

"Not your typical man from what you've told me."

"No, Charles was a suit. Business man. Lawyer. He was always in control, twenty-four seven about everything from his business to his personal life. I think that's part of the reason I let him control me so much. I'm not a strong soul."

"Yes you are, Peyton. You are one of the strongest women I know. You have to believe that about yourself. Charles broke you down with manipulation."

She blew out a long breath. "I know, but I don't trust myself where men are concerned. What if Jason turns out to be like Charles?"

"Do you really think that's true?"

"No, but what if my perception is so skewed that I can't see it?"

"You'll have to learn to trust your perception. Tell me about how Jason treats you."

Peyton glanced out the window to watch a bird flit from tree to tree. "He's kind, considerate, passionate, and he handles me with kid gloves sometimes. Other times he's in my face forcing me to meet my feelings for him head on."

"And what are your feelings for him?"

"I'm not sure." She got to her feet to wander near the doctor's bookcase to look through the volumes on behaviors in adults and children. Recognizing a few of them, she picked one up and flipped through it. Someday, she would be the one on the other side of this conversation, she vowed silently. She wanted that more than anything.

"Are you in love with him?"

"I'm not sure what love feels like. I loved Charles or thought I did and see where that got me?"

"We all are afraid to let another person become our everything, Peyton."

"He's important to me, yes."

"That's a start." The doctor wrote down something on her notepad as Peyton took the seat she'd vacated only moments before. "Do you see your future with him in or out?"

"I'd like to think he'd be in it."

"As what? Partner, lover, husband?"

"Whoa. I'm nowhere near ready for a husband."

"I didn't say you were. I asked how you saw him in your future."

"For now, lover. I'm good with that."

The doctor tapped her pen to her lips. "Somehow I don't think you are. I think you want more from him, but you're afraid to ask for it thinking he'll deny you the way Charles did."

"Jason doesn't want anything permanent, but he did ask me to marry him a couple of weeks ago."

"You didn't tell me this in our last session."

"Sorry. It was spur of the moment. He didn't mean it. I think he was feeling a little old at the time. His brother had been hurt in an auto accident and he realized he might want to think about settling down. He rescinded the offer the other night."

"It all comes down to what you want from him."

"I like having him in my life."

"Then you are wanting something more permanent than you are wanting to admit."

"Maybe." She picked at the fingernail on her right hand. Did she really want more? Something permanent like marriage? Did she love him?

"Our time is up for today. Think about what you want and what he's willing to give. He sounds like the type of guy you could do well with. Someone patient, understanding and willing to be the strong one in the relationship when it's needed, but also willing to let you be yourself. You didn't have that with Charles."

"Thanks, Doc. You've been very helpful."

"Of course. See you next week?"

"Same time, same place. I'll be here."

"Oh, how is school signups coming along?"

"Perfect. I'm all registered to take classes in a few months. It's going to be a long haul, but I need to feel like I'm helping. Being a therapist is important to me."

"I know it is." The doctor hugged her and then stepped back. "You have my complete support."

"Thanks again, Doc. You're the best."

"Call me if you need anything."

"I will."

"Good luck with Jason."

Peyton nodded as she walked out of the doctor's office and onto the street. The sun shone bright overhead, blinding her for a moment as she turned to go to her car.

A hand came down on her mouth, firmly blocking any kind of scream as a man hauled her up against his chest. "Thought I'd never find you, didn't you?"

Chapter Fourteen

Charles.

"You fucking cunt. You are the biggest worthless piece of shit I've ever had the pleasure to know."

Then why are you here?

"You're going to pay for leaving me. No one leaves me."

He dragged her to the car next to the curb in front of the doctor's office. *How the hell did he find me?*

With his hand over her throat, he cut off the oxygen to her brain. She struggled against him, realizing she would die if she didn't get away from this crazy maniac. He wouldn't have any qualms about killing her, she realized.

Jason. I never got to see him again.

Her world went dark with his face at the forefront of her mind.

When she awoke several minutes later, she gasped for breath as she tried to bring her hands to her throat, but couldn't. She was tied to a bed in a dingy hotel room. She screamed as long and as loud as she could.

"Ah, you're awake finally." He glanced around the room. "Nice, huh? About your speed I would think. I'm sure you know the place well since it's across from that shithole of a bar you work at."

Fuck. He knows where I work?

"Yes, darling. I know where you work, I know where you live, and I know who your friends are." He studied the fingernails on his left hand. "You shouldn't have run."

"I was tired of the way you were treating me. I'm not your plaything." She yanked on the rope, realizing she wouldn't get anywhere talking to him, but the bindings held tight, chafing the tender skin of her wrists.

"Oh, but you are, my dear. You are everything I want to play with until I get tired of you. You can go when that happens. For now, you're mine until I say otherwise." He watched her struggle against her bonds. "You'll only hurt yourself by doing that, Peyton."

"Let me go, Charles, and I won't press charges for kidnapping."

"I don't think anyone will miss you anytime soon. Your friends think you're headed to your fuck buddy's house tonight, do they not?"

"How?"

"You have a very active telephone line."

"You tapped my phone?"

"I have ways of listening, yes."

"You bastard! Why can't you just leave me alone? You've done enough damage already with your abuse. Find someone else to fuck up!"

He shot up out of the chair. With him looming over her, he pulled back his hand and smacked her across the right cheek. "Shut the hell up! I'm not an abuser. You just can't handle criticism at all. You never could do anything right." Her cheek stung where his ring cut into the flesh below her cheekbone. Maybe she should just keep her mouth shut and hope to get free when he left to use the bathroom or something.

He cupped her cheek with his hand as he ran his thumb across her lips. "Now see what you made me do? I don't want to hurt you, Peyton. You're everything I wanted in a woman, but you have to realize I love you and I want you to come home with me of your own freewill."

"I'll never go anywhere with you."

He sighed, moving his hand away. "So be it." He grabbed a bag off the table and pulled out a syringe. "I didn't want to have to do this, but if I have to, I will. You see, you're mine. No way around it, but you have to realize that I will take you home one way or another." He drew up whatever was in the vile into the syringe, pushing the air out the top of the needle once he withdrew it. "I'll keep you anyway I must." As he came closer, a knock sounded on the door. "Who is it?"

"The manager. I've had a complaint about noise."

Charles sighed and set the syringe down on the table, eye level with her. "I can't open the door right now, I'm not dressed, but we'll keep it down." He chuckled. "My lady friend and I just got a little carried away."

"Help me! He's keeping me hostage. Please!"

Charles slapped his hand over her mouth to muffle her cries.

"Is everything all right in there?"

"Yes, sir. My fiancé and I are playing a game of capture, is all. Nothing to be concerned about. We are into a little kinky stuff, but thank you for being concerned. It is much appreciated."

"All right. Just keep it down."

"Yes, sir."

Charles grabbed a roll of duct tape off the table, slapping a piece over her mouth before she could even take a breath to scream again.

"No more fighting me, Peyton." He tilted his head to the side. "I like the piercings and the tats. They are kind of hot."

She shot daggers at him with her gaze.

"I know. I'm such a bastard, but once I get you in the car and we're headed back to Austin, everything will be better. I can guarantee you that." He grabbed the needle from the table. "You'll sleep soundly until we reach Austin and I can take care of you. You'll love the set up I have for you, Peyton. It's private, sound proof and no one knows it's mine because I rented it. It won't be traceable at all. By the time your friends realize you're gone, I'll have you safely ensconced in our private playground where I can use you until my heart is content." After he stuck the needle deep into her thigh, he slowly pushed the medication into her. "Something to help you sleep while we travel. I know how much you hate car rides for longer than an hour." He tsked several times with his tongue. "You can be so needy."

For the second time, her world rocked on its axis as her thoughts shifted to Jason. Would she ever see him again? Would she see her friends? She never did get to go see the babies. Would anyone even miss her at all? As her thoughts jumbled, she thought she heard Jason say he loved her, but that couldn't be. Jason wasn't there.

* * * *

Jason sat in the corner of The Dusty Boot waiting for Peyton to show up for work. He'd made plans to whisk her away after her shift finished, for a fun night of debauchery, but as he glanced at his watch, he realized she was very late. He'd never known her to be late for work before. He signaled Dan at the other end of the bar. When the man moved closer, he asked if the owner knew where Peyton might be.

"Nope. She didn't show for work, which isn't like her at all. I even tried calling her phone and all I got was voicemail. Have you seen her today?"

"No. I had plans this afternoon and didn't get to talk to her."

"Have you called Mandy? Maybe she knows where she might be."

Jason snapped his fingers. "Good thought. I'll give her a call." He grabbed his cell phone from his pocket and dialed Mandy's number from his address book. He had it from before he and Peyton started seeing each other, not that he'd dated Mandy, but she'd been his contact at the feed store for getting much needed information on the equipment he needed for inseminating and storing the sperm from his bulls for use later.

The phone rang several times before she picked it up. "Hey, Jason. What's up?"

"Have you seen Peyton today?"

"I had lunch with her this afternoon and then she had an appointment at three. Why?"

"She didn't show up for work."

"What? Shit."

"What's wrong?"

"There was a creepy guy hanging around my apartment earlier just watching things. I didn't think anything of it at the time, but now I don't know. He really creeped me out. He had on a black business suit, spit shined shoes, slicked back hair. You know the type."

"Yeah, but why would that concern you?"

"She hasn't told you about Charles, has she?"

"No. Who's Charles?"

"Where are you?"

"At The Dusty Boot."

"I'll be there in twenty minutes. We need to talk."

He hung up the phone as trepidation rippled down his back. Something was wrong. He could feel it.

Several minutes later, Mandy came through the door at a dead run. "You haven't heard from her all day?"

"No, why?"

"She said she planned to call you this afternoon after her appointment."

"Who did she have an appointment with?" he asked, taking a sip from his soda on the bar. He wasn't drinking. He needed his wits about him for Peyton's sake.

"Her psychiatrist. She hasn't been seeing her that long, maybe six months?"

"She's seeing a psychiatrist? Why?"

"I have to tell you about Charles for you to understand about her seeing someone. She was with Charles for three years. She thought he was the best thing since sliced bread. Tall, rich, lawyer, and good looking to boot. She thought he would marry her and they would be this little happy family."

Jason growled.

"I'm glad you don't like the thought of that. It tells me you are in love with her as much as she is in love with you."

"She is?"

Mandy nodded as she took a sip of Jason's soda. "She is, although she doesn't want to admit it, but back to Charles. He fucked with her brain. Emotional abuse is what they call it. It's the reason she has the piercings and tats except for the one on her breast for her mother. The others she did for him because everything she did wasn't good enough. He broke down her self-esteem so bad, she wouldn't know love if it smacked her in the face. He belittled her, called her stupid and made her feel like she wasn't good enough for anyone, not even him, but then he would build her back up only to tear her down again. She left him two years ago to move here hoping the obscure remote town would fool him enough he would eventually just leave her alone. Like I said, she's been seeing the therapist for the abuse about six months now. That's who she had an appointment with this afternoon." She grabbed her phone to scroll through the numbers. "I think I have her emergency number here." She stopped, hit the button and put the phone up to her ear. After the phone clicked, she held up her finger and said, "Doctor Nash? Hi. I'm a friend of Peyton's. I know she had an appointment with you this afternoon, but have you talked to her since? No? A couple of us are concerned. She didn't show up for work. Yeah. Huh. Her car was outside your office when you left at five? That's weird. Okay. We are coming over there to check out her car and see if we can find some clues as to her whereabouts. Yeah, I know about Charles. He's a bad dude and I hope he didn't find her. Okay. Thank you." She shut the phone as she looked at Jason. "She hasn't seen her or talked to her since Peyton left her office at about three."

"Something happened to her. I just feel it. What about this Charles? Do you know anything more about him?"

"I did some digging after Peyton spilled her past to me. He practices in Austin as a criminal defense attorney."

"Figures. Do you know his last name and address? I'd like to look him up and punch the shit out of him."

"Yep. Naples is his last name and don't think I won't help you. If he hurt her, I'll kill him myself. I got an address from the internet."

Jason cracked his knuckles. "You'll be standing in line behind me, Mandy. I've already got my sights set on beating him to a pulp for what he did to her."

"Let's go check out her car so we can let the police here know what's up. She has a restraining order against the creep, but I know that doesn't mean a whole lot these days."

He followed Mandy out the door. The doctor's office wasn't far like everything in Bandera. When they reached the office, sure enough, Peyton's car sat in the parking lot beside the building. "Hmm. I don't like the looks of this. I'll call the police station. I know one of the deputies on duty tonight. Saw him checking out the patrons of the bar earlier." Jason dialed the non-emergency line at the sheriff's department.

"Bandera Sherriff's department, Officer Kailer speaking. How can I help you?"

"Hey Dillon. It's Jason Young."

"What's up, Jason?"

"My girlfriend is missing. Can you come over to—" He rattled off the address.

"Sure. Be right there."

Jason clicked the phone shut as they waited for the police to arrive. There had to be something, a clue or someone who saw her. He wandered down the block to the front door of the doctor's office looking along the sidewalk for anything he might find. Darkness surrounded the area, making it difficult to see anything out of the ordinary.

The police car pulled up near the curb, reflecting something silver on the ground. Jason bent down to see what it was, instantly recognizing the silver chain with the tiny star clasped to the end. It was Peyton's.

"So what's up, Jason?"

"My girlfriend has not been seen or heard from since this afternoon at about three. She had an appointment here at the doctor's office with her therapist. We've already talked to the doctor and she hasn't heard from her since she left. Her car is around the side of the building and she didn't show up for work tonight at The Dusty Boot."

"Her name?"

"Peyton Matthews. She has a restraining order against an old boyfriend who was abusing her."

"Did someone see her with this old boyfriend?"

"Not that we know of."

"She hasn't been missing for twenty-four hours. There isn't much I can do."

"This is her necklace she always wore." Jason held it up for the officer to see. "I found it on the sidewalk."

"She wouldn't be without it if her life depended on it," Mandy added as she stopped beside Jason. "Her mother gave her that when she knew she was dying of cancer and wouldn't be around. She never takes it off."

"We still don't have much to go on. It could have been broken and she didn't realize it. Have you called her phone?"

"Yes. It goes straight to voicemail."

"Her car hasn't been tampered with?"

"Not that we can tell."

"Sorry, Jason. There isn't much I can do. I'll take a report, but until she's been missing twenty-four hours, I can't file a missing persons report. She could be anywhere."

"Thanks for your help. I wasn't sure what you could do, but we thought we would try."

"What are you going to do from here?"

"I plan to drive to Austin tonight to check out this ex's place to see if he's seen her even if I have to beat it out of him. I need to find her."

"Be careful. You don't want to end up in jail."

"Yeah, I know and the fucker is an attorney so that would be my luck."

He and Mandy watched the officer pull away as he wondered what the hell to do now. "Where do we go from here?"

"Let's talk to the motel here in town. Maybe Charles rented a room if he was here. Wouldn't hurt."

"Okay."

They looked both ways before making their way across the street and the two blocks up to the dingy little motel in town. It was something out of a cockroach movie, but it was the only one in Bandera. If this idiot Charles stayed in town while he tried to catch up with Peyton, he would have had to stay there.

The door on the motel stood open in the summer night air as Jason and Mandy went inside. "Hey! Anyone here?" Jason rapped on the counter with his knuckles, hoping to get someone's attention.

"I'm comin'. What do you want?"

"We are looking for a friend of ours. We think he might have stayed here in town. Describe him, Mandy."

"Um, tall. Slender build. Dark hair, dark eyes. Nice looking. Probably wearing a suit and tie."

"There was a guy and a woman in the end room over yonder up until this afternoon. I saw him carry her out to the car before he drove off about six. When he checked in, he was wearing a suit. I noticed 'cause people here don't wear those expensive suits like that, you know? Not like Houston or Austin kind of highfalutin type."

"That's got to be him!" Jason slapped his hand on the desk. "Which way were they headed?"

"Out of town. He'd paid through the end of the week. Came in a couple of days ago, but he put his suitcase in the back of his car before he left, so I doubt he's coming back."

"Can we look in the room?"

"Sure, I guess. They've been gone a couple of hours." The manager grabbed the key and walked around the counter. "Follow me."

Jason almost bounced on his toes. He felt they were getting closer and closer to finding Peyton. He just hoped they would be in time before the crazy assed bastard hurt his woman in the process.

When the manager opened the door to the room, Jason and Mandy rushed inside, hoping beyond hope to find Peyton. Nothing. The room had been used from the apparent mussed bed. Jason noted the ropes tied to the headboard. This didn't look good for Peyton. What had the man done to her and what would he continue to do until they found her?

"Do you have a credit card number or anything on file in the office?" Jason asked the manager.

"He paid with cash, but he had to fill out the form with his name, address and phone number on it. I'll go get it."

"Thank you."

When the manager left, Jason inspected the ropes noting a small smear of blood on one.

"He must have drugged her."

"Why do you say that?"

Mandy held up a needle and syringe. "She wouldn't go with him willingly. I know that much."

"Is this guy crazy?"

"I think so, Jason. He didn't physically harm her before, but that doesn't mean he's beyond hurting her. I'm sure he's capable of doing anything to her to keep her, even kill her for running away."

The manager returned with the card. "Here. There's an address in Austin."

"We'll start there then," Jason said, taking the card. "Can I have this?"

"Yeah. That's a copy. I hope you find your friend."

"I hope so too."

Jason and Mandy headed back across the street to retrieve his truck. A trip to Austin would take several hours. He just hoped they'd find Peyton soon. No telling what the crazy bastard who'd taken her would do.

Once they were inside his truck, he opened the glove box and took out his .45. No telling whether he'd need it or not, but he wouldn't take the chance if they found Peyton hurt.

"You really do love her, don't you?" Mandy asked, watching him check the clip for bullets.

"Why do you say that?"

"If you didn't, you wouldn't be running off to Austin with a loaded gun to find her. Admit it Jason Young, you've fallen hard for Peyton."

He stopped for a moment as images of their time together flitted across his mind—Peyton with her hair down around her shoulders, smiling up at him, making love to her in the shower, up against the wall in his room, and across the mattress of his bed, watching her serve customers at the bar from his spot in the corner, her smile lighting up the room even from that distance. When her gaze caught his, the feeling of his stomach in his throat wouldn't go away. Yeah, he loved her. How could he not? "Yeah, I guess so."

"The stubborn fall the hardest. She's in your blood, cowboy, and you'll have no one else taking what's yours."

"Nope. He better plan on hiding well because if I have a chance at him, he'll be pushing up daisies."

"Go get 'em, cowboy!"

They drove out of Bandera hell-bent for leather to reach Austin before any harm could come to Peyton at the hands of her ex.

Chapter Fifteen

Peyton slowly opened her gritty eyes as she tried to swallow. Eating dried parchment would probably have produced more saliva. Her dried throat told her something wasn't right, but she couldn't quite put her finger on what. Everything seemed fuzzy and out of focus.

"Ah, I see you're awake finally. You slept for several hours."

Charles.

"Open those pretty little eyes for me, darling, and we'll get started on your punishment."

"Punishment?" she croaked as she tried to move, only to realize she was bound at the wrists and tied to something overhead. Her toes barely reached the floorboards. She glanced down to see he had her completely stripped of her clothing, which now lay in tatters at her feet. "What have I done?"

"You ran away, baby. I've had a terrible time finding you over the last two years. Unfortunately for you, that means my anger has grown exponentially to a rage it's been difficult to control. No one else could satisfy this need in me."

"You're crazy."

He laughed, the sound reverberated off the rafters as she glanced around. A shiver rolled down her back at the maniacal sound. This wasn't the apartment they'd rented together.

"Do you like it?" he asked, his gaze sweeping the room. "It's roomier. I got it especially for you and me to get reacquainted in now that I can release the inner beast I've been holding back. Something I can easily do since I've been planning this for such a long time."

"Inner beast?"

"Darling, darling, darling." He cupped her face with his palm. "You haven't seen anything from me yet. I didn't want to frighten you before by playing with you the way I wanted to, so I spent time with others to sate my desires, but now it'll be all on you."

He reached into a duffle bag sitting on the floor near her feet. A long leather whip unfurled when he pulled it out.

"What are you going to do with that?"

"Mark up your pretty body so you'll know you belong to me. Only my mark will be forever etched into your brain."

"Mark?"

"I've become quite the master at the bullwhip. I can leave nothing more than a small red spot or I can draw blood, depending on your responses."

"Listen, Charles. I'm sorry I ran, but I didn't know what to do. You were so distant. If you let me go, I'll be the perfect lover for you. I'll do anything you want me to do. I won't run again, I promise."

"Tsk, tsk, tsk. I'm sorry, but I don't believe you anymore, Peyton. You've lied to me, ran from me, cheated on me, and disappointed me beyond repair." He placed his hand over his heart. "Now you'll pay for your misdeeds until I say you've had enough."

He stepped behind her, trailing the whip over her back, leaving goose bumps along her flesh.

"You know, your skin will mark nicely. I haven't had a woman who had skin the color of yours. Black women don't mark so well. White woman are beautiful to mark although I wasn't too picky with those I've taken." He shrugged as he continued to trail the whip over her skin.

"Please, Charles. Just let me go. I won't report anything. I won't tell a soul."

"Sorry. I can't do that, Peyton. You need to be punished." He moved behind her, cracking the whip into the air.

She jumped as tears started to roll down her cheeks. He'd never been physical before, but apparently he'd been saving that little piece of information from her for some time. It was only the emotional abuse she'd had to endure. Now it would be physical too.

The first sting of the whip on her skin made her jump, but it didn't hurt too much, not anymore than the needle from a piercing or tattoo. However, there was a difference in this pain. It wasn't self-inflicted. The piercings and tats helped her deal with the self-loathing, low self-esteem and emotional distress the abuse from Charles had inflicted. The burning slash of the whip didn't make her feel better.

"Charles, stop!"

Having him inflict pain that had nothing to do with pleasure, made it abuse, and she wasn't going to tolerate this from him anymore.

"Oh, baby. You have no idea how far I'm willing to take you."

The whip struck again. This time, she could feel the blood seeping from the wound on her shoulder. He was a monster, crazy beyond anything she'd ever dealt with before.

Before long, he was constantly taking the whip to her back as she tried to disconnect her mind from the pain. He laughed as he stopped for a moment to touch one of the wounds. A scream tore from her throat as the salt from his skin penetrated the wound.

The door burst open as her head swam. "Jason?" Her voice came out in a painful whisper.

"Back away slowly."

"Who the hell are you and what are you doing in my house?"

"I've come for Peyton."

"She's mine to do with as I wish. Leave now before I have you arrested for trespassing."

"She's not yours, she's mine, you bastard, and you can't have her."

Charles coiled the whip.

"Jason!" Peyton yelled, seconds too late as the whip struck his wrist, pulling the pistol from his grasp and sending it skidding across the floor. Charles struck again, landing a slice across Jason's cheek.

Jason dove at Charles as Peyton twisted around trying to keep them in her sights. A set of hands worked at the knots at her wrists. "No! I need to make sure Jason is all right. Leave me. Help him."

"Hush. Jason can handle himself."

"Mandy?"

"Easy, honey. I'll have you down in a minute." Mandy grumbled under her breath about Charles being a bastard and she'd cut his balls off should she get the chance.

The two men struggled on the floor, rolling around, knocking over furniture in their struggle to get the upper hand. "I'll kill you for hurting her."

"She's mine, cowboy, and nothing you can do to stop me. She's my wife."

"Wife?"

"Yes. We were married this evening when we reached Austin."

"Peyton?" Mandy asked.

"I don't know, Mandy. It's a blur from when I left the doctor's office. He was drugging me."

Jason climbed to his feet, breathing hard from the struggle with Charles. Unfortunately, now Charles had the gun and the bullwhip.

"Charles, please. Let them go. I'll do whatever you want," she implored with her hands out as she slowly walked toward him.

"I need to kill them, just like the others, so they can't point fingers at me."

"Others?"

"The women. The ones I used before I found you. They had to die. All of them."

Mandy and Jason looked at each other and then back at Peyton. "They won't say anything, Charles, right Jason?"

"Are you crazy? He just admitted he killed God only knows how many people. He needs to go to jail, Peyton."

"But if you don't say anything, he'll let you go, won't you, Charles? It's your word against theirs that you said anything. You're an attorney. You know the evidence is threadbare."

"They have to die."

She stepped closer, hoping she could get the gun out of his hands or keep him from shooting the two people who meant the world to her. "They'll go. Right guys? Just leave. Go back to Bandera."

"I'm not leaving without you, Peyton."

"Me either."

"Stubborn asses! Go!" She got close enough to see the confusion in Charles' eyes. He really was crazy. "Give me the gun, Charles."

"No. I have to kill them."

"Charles, please, let them go and I'll do whatever you want. I'll stay with you forever."

Charles waved the gun toward Jason, pointing at his chest. "I must kill them or they'll find us again."

He took aim at Jason. Just as he pulled the trigger, Peyton swung, hitting the gun in his hand as she prayed Jason hadn't been hit.

"You bitch!" The gun came up in her face as she stared down the barrel of a .45 pointed between her eyes. "You'll die with them!"

A blur rushed into Charles' side as Jason tackled them both. She screamed out in pain as her back hit the wooden floor.

Jason and Charles wrestled for the gun now trapped between their bodies. An explosion cracked the air and Peyton screamed once more.

* * * *

Jason wrestled with Charles across the floor. The gun trapped between their bodies. This wouldn't turn out well, one way or another, but if it meant Peyton would be safe, then so be it. He would give his life to keep her out of this maniac's hands.

Peyton screamed as the gun went off.

Jason waited for the burn of the bullet as it penetrated his body, but it never came.

He looked down in Charles' wide eyes.

The other man didn't move, his gaze fixed to the ceiling above them in death's blank stare.

"Jason!"

"I'm okay," he said as he moved back, taking the gun from the dead man's hands.

Blood seeped across Charles' chest, spreading over the entire front of his shirt.

"Mandy, call the police," Jason said, stepping back as Peyton threw herself into his arms.

"Already on it," she replied, talking into her cell phone as she gave them the information on where they were located.

"Are you okay?" he asked, pushing her back a little so he could unbutton his shirt.

"You know I love to see your chest, Jason, but really? Is now a good time?"

"Baby, you need something on."

She glanced down at her exposed chest and crossed her arms over her naked breasts. "Oh yeah." He wrapped his shirt around her, helping her to stuff her arms into the sleeves. She hissed as the shirt touched her back.

"You'll be going to the hospital to get those looked at."

"I'm fine." She grabbed him around the waist the moment he finished buttoning up the front of the shirt. "Hold me."

"No problem, darlin'. I'll hold you as long as you want me to."

"Don't ever leave. I need you."

"Honey, you've got me wrapped around your little finger. I'm not goin' anywhere."

Within several minutes, the police arrived with guns drawn. Jason had placed his gun on the bare coffee table across the room and sat with Peyton on the couch trying to calm her shaking as the rush of everything hit her.

"The ambulance is here too."

"He doesn't need one, but she does."

"I'm fine."

"No you aren't, darlin'. You'll let them take a look at your back," he said, holding her as close as he could. He almost lost her and the thought scared the hell out of him. "She's been whipped."

"Let's see so we can evaluate you, ma'am," the paramedic said as she slowly unbuttoned the shirt. "We need to take you in so the doctor can look at those. Some are pretty deep."

She glanced at Jason. "You'll go with me?"

"Of course. I'm not leaving your side if I don't have to."

"Thank you for rescuing me."

"I love you. There is no place I'd rather be."

"You love me?"

"Yes. This isn't the time or place for this conversation, but I do love you and I hope you love me too."

"I do, Jason. I love you so much." She buried her face in his neck and he felt the warm trickle of tears on his skin.

"Ma'am?"

"All right." She wiped the tears from her eyes as she sat back.

Her tears broke his heart. He never wanted to see them again on her pretty face. "There now." He wiped the remaining wetness from her cheeks. "Let's get you fixed up."

"I'll need your statement, sir," one of the officers said, as his partner called the coroner's office. "It appears this is self-defense, but we'll need to get the detectives involved."

"No problem."

"It'll have to be after he gets checked out," the paramedic replied, indicating the small amount of blood on his left side. "It appears you've been shot, sir."

"It's just a flesh wound."

"What? You were shot? Let me see." Peyton turned him so she could inspect the trench dug through his flesh. "Jason, you need to get checked too. This could be serious."

"He missed."

"Not entirely."

"Fine. We'll go together."

"We'll get your statement at the hospital then, sir."

Mandy stepped forward toward the officer. "I'm a witness to what happened. I'll stay and give you a statement too."

The paramedics ushered the two of them out to the waiting ambulance and into the back. Jason insisted they put Peyton on the stretcher on her side so she could relax and he would sit in the front.

He called his parents on the way to the hospital to fill them in on what was happening. "No Mom, I'm fine. It's a flesh wound, but I'm going to have the doctor look at it to make sure it doesn't need anything besides a bandage. Peyton's wounds need to be looked at too. We'll probably stay here in Austin for a couple of days because the police will want to talk to us, I'm sure. No, we'll be okay. You don't need to come. Just do me a favor, call Dan at The Dusty Boot and let him know what is going on so he doesn't get more worried than he is. Have someone check my animals please.

Thanks Mom. I love you too and yes, I'll hug Peyton for you. Bye."

Shortly after the sun broke over the horizon, they drove into the ambulance bay at the hospital, the paramedics ushered them both inside into separate rooms, but only sectioned off by a curtain. He asked them to leave it open and even though the nurse seemed reluctant, she did what he asked.

Peyton's wounds weren't too deep, but the doctor had to stitch a few closed. The others would heal on their own. She would have scars to match the wounded soul he now knew lie within. Mandy had told him about the hell she'd went through living with this guy. He knew he would spend the rest of his life making sure she knew she was the most beautiful woman inside and out, he'd ever seen.

"You okay over there?" he asked from across the room.

"Yeah," she replied, her voice small and broken.

He got off the gurney so he could move to her side. "Baby, don't. Don't let him win. He was totally wrong about you."

"I can't help it, Jason. I spent years listening to him tell me how worthless I am. How ugly things were between us. How I couldn't satisfy him in bed…"

"Baby, you're gorgeous. You have a wonderful life. You are going to school in the fall to help people in situations just like yours. You are the most amazing woman I've ever had in my bed. I'll hear no more about all of this. He's gone. He's dead. He can't hurt you anymore and believe me when I say I will spend the rest of my life making sure you know how much you mean to me."

"Did you really mean it when you said you loved me?"

"Of course, I meant it. The minute I get the chance, we're going to get married."

"Married? You want to marry me?"

"Yeah. I want you with me forever."

"Married," she whispered, tears making her eyes sparkle like golden topaz. "I never thought I'd hear those words from you again after you said it before. You aren't the marrying kind, remember?"

"I am now—with you." He leaned in and kissed her. Not a quick peck, but a full onslaught of desire waiting to explode between them at the merest touch. "I love you."

"I love you too."

The doctor cleared his throat as he came into the room. "You two can leave as soon as I get the nurse to dress the wounds."

"Thanks, Doc."

"You're welcome. I hope the guy who did this to her won't be hurting anyone else?"

"No sir, he won't."

"Good and I don't care who hears me say it either."

While they were waiting for their discharge papers, the police came in and told them they would have to come to the station tomorrow morning to make their statements.

"That's fine, officer. We don't plan to leave town for a couple of days if you need us to be here."

"We aren't going home?"

"No, I told my mom to have the guys keep an eye on my cattle and horses for me. We'll stay here a couple of days."

Mandy came through the doorway with a smile. "Everything is good. I'm going to take the bus on home to leave you two some time to get reacquainted."

"Thanks, Mandy, for everything," Peyton said as she hugged her.

"Can you take my truck to the store a few blocks away and get her something to wear besides my shirt, before you go? We'll take you to the bus stop after they release us."

"Okay."

Mandy took his keys, whistling happily as she twirled the key ring around her finger. "I'll be back."

"Don't wreck my truck."

"I won't, cowboy. I like big things." She laughed as she skipped down the hallway.

He took the seat next to the gurney to await their discharge papers. "You can move in with me when we get back."

"But your house isn't even finished yet."

"I know, but you'll be able to decorate it however you want. I'd love to have your help on how certain things should be in the house since it'll be your house now too."

"I like the sound of that."

"You plan to continue your therapy, right? I think you need to so you can work through what happened last night and yesterday."

"Yes, I will. This has all taken me back a step in my recovery, but with you by my side, I can overcome anything."

"That's right. I'll be there for you every step of the way."

"You know I love you, right?"

"I'm glad to hear you say it because you mean everything to me, Peyton. You've become someone very important in my life. I'll do everything I need to do to help you. You own my heart."

"Are you two ready to go?" the nurse asked as she came into the room. "I have your discharge papers here."

"Good."

Once the nurse went through the instructions with each of them after she dressed their wounds, she had them sign the papers and then escorted them out to the waiting room.

"A friend has gone to get her some clothes."

"Just hand the scrubs back to the receptionist before you leave."

"We will. Thank you." He shook the nurse's hand. "We appreciate everything you've done."

"No problem. That's what we are here for."

A few minutes later, Mandy came through the door with a couple of bags of clothes. "I didn't get anything fancy. Just a shirt, jeans. I grabbed your shoes from the house. He didn't ruin those."

"Thanks, Mandy. You're the best." Peyton hugged her quickly and then took the clothes into the nearby bathroom while they waited.

"How's she really doing?" Mandy asked.

"Broken. She needs to talk to her therapist right away. That asshole brought back way too much stuff buried inside her soul."

"So when's the wedding?" Mandy asked, rubbing her hands together in glee.

Jason smiled and shook his head. "Soon, I hope."

Mandy threw her arms around his neck and hugged him tight. "I knew you two were good for each other."

"Thanks."

"Hey, that's my fiancé you are hanging all over." Peyton stopped at their side with her fresh new tank top, jeans, and tennis shoes.

"I know! I think it's totally cool you two are planning to get married. Jason won't tell me when the wedding is, but I better be a maid of honor."

"Of course you will be. We can't give you a date because he just asked me like ten minutes ago."

"Well, I'll leave you two alone. I'm taking a cab to the bus station."

"I told you we'd take you."

"No problem. You two go on and have fun. Be careful with her, she's been through a lot," Mandy scolded as she shook her finger at him

"I will. No hanky panky. I just plan to hold her very tight."

"Good. I'll see you two in a couple of days."

"Thanks again. For everything," Peyton said, hugging her friend for a moment as tears sparkled on her eyelashes. Mandy only hugged her shoulders as she tried not to touch her back. He began to love her even more for her care. "I don't know what I would have done had you and Jason not come to find me."

"Stop. You'll make me cry too." Mandy stepped back, shooing Peyton into his arms. "I love you both." Mandy disappeared out the doors, leaving he and Peyton standing alone.

"Shall we go find a hotel room?"

One eyebrow shot up over Peyton's eye. "Can we have sex?"

"Baby, I don't think that's a good idea with your back."

"You're probably right." She shivered next to him. "We should probably get something to eat before we find a hotel. I'm starving."

"Considering it's about noon, I'm not surprised. I saw a burger joint not far from here."

"Sounds good." She grabbed his hand as they headed outside to his truck.

He knew having sex with her could be bad for her physically, but emotionally, he wasn't sure. He didn't do emotions very well. He wasn't sure if his own could handle a breakdown from her if it occurred, but he would tough it out. She would need him tonight. Her emotions would be fragile with the torture her ex dealt out. Holding her close might help when things came to a head.

Chapter Sixteen

They made the short trip to the burger joint and ordered what they wanted. As they waited for their food to come, he took her hands between his. A kiss to each fingertip made his cock stand up to take notice. *Down boy.* "How are you feeling?"

"Sore."

"What about what's going on in that brain of yours?"

"I'm not sure I know what you mean."

"Baby, you just went through something that would fuck up someone's emotions even on their best day. I know what happened had to have brought back a lot of memories."

She grasped his hands like a lifeline as her knuckles turned white. "Charles didn't abuse me physically before. Apparently, he was holding back that little bit of information from me when he was fucking with my head. Yes, it's hard for me to wrap my brain around it right now because I didn't see this coming. I should have. Many times when someone abuses on an emotional level, the physical is there too, but he didn't, at least not in the past."

He gently rubbed his thumb over the back of her hand until her death grip eased.

"Easy, baby. I will never let anyone hurt you again. He's gone. Dead. He can't hurt you anymore." Why he brought this up here, he wasn't sure. He shouldn't have. "I'm sorry. We can talk about this later when we are alone."

"Okay. I'm going to need to talk, Jason. I've got to let these emotions out and I don't want to do it here in the restaurant."

"It's fine." The waitress brought their food, easing the plates onto the table in front of them. Peyton took a deep breath and dove into her food like a starving woman. Jason squirted some ketchup on his plate for his fries as he kept an eye on his woman. She needed him to be strong for her and he would be. "Let's talk about something else for now. We can get into the emotional turmoil when we get to the hotel. When would you like to get married?"

"Are you sure you want to marry me?"

"I love you, Peyton. Of course, I want to marry you."

"How is your family going to feel about you taking on such a project?"

"My family will love you. My mother already does from what she's told me even though she will want to get to know you better."

"What are they going to say? We haven't really known each other very long."

"Long enough to know I want you in my life. When I found your car at the doctor's office and didn't know where to find you, my heart settled in my stomach. I knew then I loved you because I couldn't think of my life without you in it. If I'd lost you, I would've gone nuts. You are the most important person to me."

"Have I told you I love you?"

"Yes, but I like hearing it. Up to a few months ago, I thought finding the perfect person for me was impossible. I told myself I would stop using women for my own pleasure. You were a test of my abilities because you wanted to have casual sex. I gave into that mentality even though it went against what I'd vowed to change, because I wanted you so badly, I would have done anything to have you." He smiled as her eyes widened. "I've been watching you for several months while you worked the bar, trying to figure out a way to get closer to you. When you showed up at the muddin' party with Aaron, I wanted to rip his throat out."

She laughed. "You did?"

"Yeah, because I thought for sure you were going home with him and he would be getting what I wanted."

"You only wanted me for sex?"

"No, well yeah. Sort of." He popped the last of his hamburger into his mouth. While he chewed, he tried to decide how to tell her at first he wanted sex, but after he'd gotten to know her, it had turned into more. "You see, all I've ever known with a woman is sex. I hadn't wanted anything more until you, but when I thought of you with Aaron, I wanted to be him. I wanted what he was going to have. I didn't know what type of relationship you had with him and it bugged me. When you got into the fight with him and turned to me, it was like my entire world lit up. This is why I resisted so hard when we first started talking that night. I realized I wanted a little more from you than just sex. I wanted to hold you, touch you and love on you all night. I wanted to wake up next to you in the morning so I could see the sunlight touch your hair. I wanted your eyes to light up when you saw me like they do now. You are my world now, Peyton."

A tear rolled down her cheek and he reach across the table to wipe it away. "Sorry."

"Why are you crying?"

"Because I never thought I'd find a love like yours, especially with a cowboy. You've tempted me beyond reason to let love find us. I never thought I would fall for a cowboy." She laughed as she wiped another tear with her napkin, smearing ketchup across her cheek.

"Why not? You don't like cowboys, but you live in Texas?" he asked, laughing with her as he reached over with his own napkin to wipe the red from her face.

"I've certainly learned to love one cowboy—you."

"Good, because I love you so much, I can't think of anyone else anymore." He pushed his plate away. "All finished?"

"Yes." She bit her lip as a frown settled across her brow.

"What's wrong?"

"What about Sheila?"

"What about her?"

"She said she's pregnant with your child."

"I found out from her the other day, she's only two months along or so she says. There is no way she's pregnant with my child. We weren't together in the right time frame."

"Thank God."

"Ready to settle in for the night?"

"Yeah."

"Let's go find us a room then. I want to hold you."

After they finished paying the check, they walked back out to his truck and he opened the door for her. As soon as she was settled in, he went back around the front to the driver's side. They would have a nice room. No dive dump for them tonight. If he could swing the softest bed in the city, he would. "Where do you want to stay?"

"Nothing too expensive, Jason. You need to save your money."

"We'll have a nice room for the days we are here and I'll hear no more about it. You deserve something nice. Maybe a Jacuzzi tub?"

She smiled and he got the impression she liked the idea of a whirlpool tub in their room. He kind of did too. Maybe she'd let him fuck her in it.

He pulled out his phone to check on some hotels nearby. He loved a smart phone. He found a Marriott nearby so he headed in that direction. They were usually a good bet for nice rooms even though they might not have the jetted tub. "We'll go here first and see if they have something."

"Are you sure? Those are expensive."

"Nothing is too good for my girl."

"I think you're going to spoil me something terrible." A smile eased up the corners of her mouth.

He loved to make her smile, moan, groan or scream. Man was he in trouble. This not having sex with her would kill him slowly. "I get to. You're my woman now."

They pulled into the hotel and he looked up at the high-rise. *This should be perfect.*

When they walked through the lobby, he saw all the marble accents and wondered briefly if his wallet could afford a room here for a couple of days, but decided it didn't matter. She was worth every penny. "Do you have rooms with whirlpool tubs in them?"

"Yes, sir."

"I need one for two nights, please," he told the man behind the desk. He swore his credit card groaned as they swiped it for the charges.

"Are you sure about this, Jason? That's a lot of money."

"Very sure."

"You are in twenty-four forty-five. It's a suite on twenty-fourth floor."

"Thank you," Jason said, as he took the key card.

"Do you have luggage?"

"No."

The clerk's eyebrow rose. "I see."

"This was an unexpected trip. We'll be doing some shopping in the morning."

"Very good, sir."

They headed for the elevator to go to their room. "I feel so cheap. That guy thinks this is a hook up."

"Don't worry about him, baby. We'll get some clothes for both of us and a suitcase. It doesn't matter what he thinks, it only matters what we know." He grinned as he slipped his arm around her waist, trying not to touch the sores on her back. "We can do some engagement ring shopping too."

"I can't believe we're going to get married."

He lifted her hand to his lips and kissed her palm. "Believe it. I love you with all my heart."

"I love you too."

The door opened to the twenty-fourth floor. As they walked down the carpeted hallway, he was in awe. There were only three doors along the whole thing. The deskman had said it was a suite, but holy shit! He found their door, then swiped the key before he pushed it open. "Wow."

They walked inside and let the door close behind them as they stood with their mouths open at the grandeur of the room. "Oh my God, Jason. This is gorgeous!" She walked around touching the marble with her fingers, the crystal on the lamps and the cherry wood tables. "Look at this view!" A large bank of windows looked out over the city. "I've never seen Austin like this."

"Me either, but I can imagine you against these windows with your hands braced against the glass as I fuck you from behind."

"If you aren't going to do it, don't tease me like that."

"But just think, tomorrow it'll be better with the anticipation."

"Asshole." She laughed as she spun around and wrapped her arms around his neck. "I love you."

"I love you too. Shall we get some sleep?"

"Yeah. I find I'm really tired now that things are calm."

"Good. I hope you can rest without nightmares or anything."

"If you hold me, I should be fine."

He eased the tank top over her head, revealing her bare breasts. "Did she get some sexy-ass underwear?"

"Yes," she whispered, her breath coming out in short, panting bursts of air. "I want you."

"I want you too, but for now and tonight, I'm just going hold you."

"But…"

"No, buts, darlin'. You need to ease into this again. You had a rough time."

"I know what I want, Jason."

"I know, but we just rest tonight. I have a feeling you're going have a rough night." He stripped off his shirt and T-shirt. She touched his chest, earning herself a moan from his lips. He loved when she let her fingers walk along his skin. He grabbed her hands to stop the motion.

"I only want to touch."

"I know, but your skin on mine is something I can't handle too much of. Holding you without lovin' you is going to be hard enough."

"Party pooper." She pouted with her lip stuck out.

"It's for your own good, darlin'," he said, tapping the end of her nose with his fingertip.

"Okay." She stripped off her jeans, leaving her in nothing but her lacy panties. "I'll sleep in my underwear, but since you are declaring this no sex night, you'll have to suck it up, cowboy."

When she turned to pull down the blankets, the stark whiteness of the bandages on her back made him want to kill the son of a bitch all over again.

They both crawled beneath the covers and he dragged her into his embrace with an arm around her shoulders so he wouldn't touch her back. He wanted to feel her next to him like he needed his next breath.

Within minutes, her breathing slowed to a rhythmic rate indicating she slept. When he thought about what that asshole did to her, rage swept through him. He would die protecting her for the rest of his life.

The feel of her against his side lulled him into a half sleepy state. He knew the night would be rough on her so he slept lightly waiting for the storm of nightmares he felt sure would assault her soon.

He came upright in the bed as she screamed out in her sleep. "Baby, wake up."

"No! Don't hurt me!"

"Peyton, it's me. I'll never hurt you, sweetheart. Wake up."

She jumped out of the bed with her fists clenched and her eyes wide. "Jason?"

"Yeah, baby. It's me. Come back to bed. He can't hurt you anymore."

"Oh God." She scrambled onto the bed, practically jumping into his arms.

"Easy." He swept his hands down her arms, rubbing the warmth back into her limbs. "I love you." Once he pulled her into his embrace, she settled against his side. Her body still shook from the nightmare. "Why don't you tell me about your dream?"

"I was back in that room. He cut off my clothes with a knife, slicing my skin as he did it. The pain was too much, but as I cried, he'd just laugh." She shuddered. "His laughter was crazy. Then he started whipping me so hard, I screamed. That's when I woke up."

"It's over, baby. He's dead."

She pulled him closer. "I know, but I think these nightmares will continue for a bit."

"Probably."

"I know you don't want to make love, but I need you, Jason. I need you to wipe out the memory of what I've been through. We can go easy. I'll be on top or whatever."

"If you think you can handle it."

"I do. I need you to replace all these terrible thoughts with your love. Please?"

"Oh, baby, I'll love you so well, you won't remember what his face looks like." He shifted, leaving her on her side so he could reach her breasts. *Lordy, I so love her breasts.* "These are perfect, you know."

"Are they?"

"Yep. I love how they fit perfectly in my palms." He cupped the two mounds as he licked first the right, then the left. "And your nipples are so sensitive."

She moaned as she closed her eyes. He loved that look of ecstasy on her face as she let the feelings envelope her in sensation.

He let his hand wander down her abdomen as she spread her thighs allowing him touch her. He loved feeling her pussy clench around his fingers when he slipped two inside her. She felt so good, he wanted to taste her.

He moved down her body with little nips on her skin until he reached the juncture of her thighs. He lifted one leg over his shoulder so he could reach her center. The smell of her arousal drove him crazy. One swipe of his tongue over her clit made her groan out loud.

"Please."

He flicked his tongue over the hardened little button of flesh, coaxing it from its hiding place until she squirmed against his mouth seeking a little more pressure so she could come. The soft whimpers and hearty moans told him she was close. To let her come or not, was the question.

Nope. He wanted to be buried deep inside her pussy when she flew apart in his arms.

He lifted his head, ignoring her protests.

"I have an idea. Up you go." With her hand in his, he pulled her to the bank of windows overlooking the city of Austin. "I'm gonna fuck you against the windows."

"But people will see us."

"Do you care? Besides, being dark inside our room, they won't be able to see anything, but what if they do?" He pushed her against the glass, her back to his front although he didn't touch her open wounds. "Your beautiful breasts squashed against the windowpane, the nipples hard from the cooler surface." He ran his tongue down her neck and across her shoulder before he bit the flesh. "Your gorgeous thighs spread for my use, my cock pushed up inside you so deep, you moan with pleasure." He licked across the flesh of her shoulder. "Do you want me, Peyton? Do you want me to fuck you here where everyone could possibly see us?"

"Yes, damn you."

"Ah, such a naughty little girl." He pressed two fingers into her pussy from behind as she spread her thighs. "You're horny just thinking about someone across the way being able to see you getting fucked like this."

"Give it to me."

"In a minute." He finger fucked her for several minutes as she pressed herself against the glass. "I want to make sure you're good and ready for me."

She moaned. "I'm ready. Trust me."

"Feel that cold glass against your breasts. Are your nipples hard from it?"

"Yes."

"Are you wet?"

"Hell yes. Please, Jason."

He dropped his pants and stepped out of the jeans and underwear, then pressed his aching cock against her backside. "Do you want me?"

"Oh yeah."

"Spread your thighs, baby, I'm coming home." He pressed closer, careful to keep his chest away from her wounds as he nudged at her opening from behind.

"God, you're going to feel amazing." He pushed his cock into her pussy very slowly. "Fuck yeah."

The heat from her scorched his cock, driving his need higher than he'd ever felt before. They probably should have used a condom, but since they were getting married anyway, he didn't really care if she got pregnant and he knew they were both clean from their conversation before. "Did the hospital ask about rape?"

"Yes, but he didn't," she whispered. "I think he planned on it after he beat me senseless, but you saved me before that happened."

"God, you feel amazing." He shuddered, absorbing the intenseness of being deep inside her. He slowly made love to her against the glass, giving her the security he felt she needed that he loved her and would always protect her from her demons. "I love you. I will always love you. You are everything to me." He slipped inside her, holding himself still until she squirmed with need. "Do you want control?"

"Yes."

He picked her up as he backed toward the bed to lie down. "Reverse cowgirl, baby. Take what you want. You're in control." She slid herself back over his cock, moaning softly as she impaled herself with his entire length. Bracing herself on his thighs, she began a torturous slow glide of his cock in and out of her amazingly hot pussy. "You're going to kill me, darlin'."

"But what a way to go."

She did a slow grind of her pussy against him, driving him insane with lust. "Fuck me, baby."

"Oh I plan to."

With a shift of her hips, she rocked back and forth on him, letting his cock slide in and out of her pussy in the most insanely erotic dance of his life. She started working her clit with her fingertip as she kept up a steady pace with her hips.

When he couldn't stand it anymore, he flipped her over onto her stomach over the edge of the bed and slammed into her with enough force to bang the headboard against the wall.

"I wondered when you would take over, cowboy. I figured it wouldn't take long. You don't like not being in control."

"I'm going to fuck you into next week."

"Do it!"

He slammed his pelvis against her and felt her pussy squeeze his cock almost in two. His rhythm became disjointed as he continued to push his cock into her heated flesh in a rapid pace. He couldn't hold out much longer, but she needed to come along for the ride.

Knowing she needed a little more stimulation, he wrapped his hand around her hip so he could reach her clit. When he touched the hard little button, she growled in satisfaction. He smiled even though he knew she couldn't see the satisfied grin on his face.

"Right there."

"Oh yeah."

With two fingers, he pinched her clit and she came apart on a scream of his name. Her pussy clamped down on him so hard, it almost hurt, but felt amazing at the same time as he lost his load deep inside her.

He collapsed on the bed in a heap, allowing his cock to slide from her depths. "That was fantastic."

"Thank you."

"Can we do it again?"

He laughed as he reached down to kiss her shoulder. "Give me a little bit to recover and we'll love the night away."

"You are my forever."
"And you are mine."

Epilogue

The early spring morning was perfect for a wedding. Peyton just hoped the rain would hold off since the sky looked a bit threatening at times.

Jason had been her everything from the day he'd found her at the hands of Charles, giving her time, space and love. She couldn't have asked for a better husband or lover. He was so patient and understanding with her nightmares and mood swings, but the weekly visits to the therapist had the nightmares down to only infrequently now.

Nina stood next to her as they fluffed her veil, settling it around her shoulders in preparation for her to walk down the aisle. "You look beautiful."

She hugged Jason's mother close as tears threatened to smear her makeup.

"No tears or you'll ruin my makeup job!" Mandy exclaimed, pushing her into the chair so she could finish with the veil.

"Thank you all for everything. I'm sorry my own mother isn't here to see this day, but you all have made me feel so welcomed into the family, I can't thank you enough."

Nina sniffed as she wiped a tear from the corner of her eye. "You are perfect for my son and I'm glad I could help make this day the most special day for you two."

Mesa sat beside her in one of the wing back chairs in the room they were using for the wedding party at the ranch. She almost didn't make the wedding since she was very pregnant with her and Joel's first child.

"Are you okay?" Peyton asked Mesa as she rubbed her bulging stomach.

"I'm fine, just tired. I wish this little one would hurry up and make its appearance. I'm already overdue."

"Only a few days, Mesa," Nina added. "I was two weeks overdue with Jeff. First babies are very difficult to judge."

"Well, I'm ready anytime."

The girls laughed, knowing she was really getting tired of being pregnant. "You'll be a great mom, Mesa," Paige said, as she stood in the corner to look out the window.

Peyton loved having her friends with her on this very important day. "I'm not sure if Jason and I will have children."

"Do you want them?" Nina asked.

"I think so, but with all the trauma in my life, I'm not sure if I could handle them."

"No hurry. You and Jason are still young enough to decide later and with all of my new grandbabies, I can wait a little while for more."

They all laughed.

There was a soft knock on the door. Nina moved toward it to see who it was. The ceremony would be starting soon so she thought it might be Jason's father. She'd asked him to give her away since her own father wasn't in the picture.

James came through the door, looking dapper in his tuxedo shirt, black jacket and tie along with his black jeans and black boots. He wore the same outfit her husband would when they took their vows in a few short minutes.

Her stomach lurched. Was she ready for this?

Nina and James came to stand behind her. "He loves you, Peyton. You love him. You'll be very happy together." Nina glanced at James. "Just like we are as well as the others are. You'll fit in perfectly." She squeezed her fingers. "Welcome to the family."

"Are you ready? It's about time to start," James said taking her hand in his. "Your fingers are like ice."

"I'm a little nervous."

"Perfectly normal for your wedding day. You look beautiful."

"Thank you for standing in to give me away."

"It's my pleasure."

He looped her hand through the crook of his arm as she stood and faced her wedding party. Her bridesmaids looked beautiful in their teal off the shoulder dresses. Mandy wore the same style but in a deep burgundy red.

Everything was perfect.

"Ready?" James asked as he led her toward the door to follow the other women down the stairs.

"Yes."

When the wedding march started several minutes later, she swallowed, took in a deep breath and prepared to meet the man of her dreams in front of the fireplace at Thunder Ridge Ranch.

As they reached the bottom of the stairs, she took in the entire main lodge decorated for her wedding. Her wedding to Jason. The thought scared her and excited her at the same time.

As the crowd parted, she got her first look at her future husband in his finery. He took her breath away, but the one thing that made her heart stop was the look in his eyes as their gazes met across the room.

The love shining in his eyes almost brought her to her knees, causing her to stumble slightly.

"You okay?" James whispered as they made their way toward Jason.

"Yeah."

When they reached Jason's side and his father gave her over to him, she couldn't help but thank God above for tempting her with this cowboy and bringing them together for all eternity.

"I love you."

"I love you too."

"Ready to get married?"

"I've never been more ready for anything in my life."

The End

About the Author

Sandy Sullivan is a romance author, who, when not writing, spends her time with her husband Shaun on their farm in middle Tennessee. She loves to ride her horses, play with their dogs and relax on the porch, enjoying the rolling hills of her home south of Nashville. Country music is a passion of hers and she loves to listen to it while she writes.

She is an avid reader of romance novels and enjoys reading Nora Roberts, Jude Deveraux and Susan Wiggs. Finding new authors and delving into something different helps feed the need for literature. A registered nurse by education, she loves to help people and spread the enjoyment of romance to those around her with her novels. She loves cowboys so you'll find many of her novels have sexy men in tight jeans and cowboy boots.

Other books by Sandy

Love Me Once, Love Me Twice (Montana Cowboys 1)
Before the Night is Over (Montana Cowboys 2)
Two for the Price of One (Montana Cowboys 3)
Difficult Choices (Montana Cowboys 4)
Doctor Me Up (Montana Cowboys 5)
Stakin' His Claim
Country Minded Cougar

Meet Me in the Barn
Taming the Cougar
The Call of Duty Anthology
Five Hearts Anthology
Trouble With a Cowboy
Gotta Love a Cowboy
Make Mine a Cowboy (Cowboy Dreamin' 1)
Healing a Cowboy's Heart (Cowboy Dreamin' 2)
For the Love of a Cowboy (Cowboy Dreamin' 3)

Secret Cravings Publishing
www.secretcravingspublishing.com